I0567682

Oracle's Vision

Wiccan Haus Book 19

By
TL Reeve & Michele Ryan

Copyright © 2016 by TL Reeve & Michele Ryan
ISBN: 978-1-68361-137-0
Cover art by Fiona Jayde

Published by
Decadent Publishing Company, LLC

Look for us online at:
www.decadentpublishing.com

~A Note from the Authors~

Dear Readers,

Thank you for picking up a copy of Oracle's Vision. We hope you enjoy reading it as much as we enjoyed writing it. Nai, Cade and Amanda have an interesting story, and trust me there were several more stories Nai could have told us. The few that are woven through our story are just a few of the interesting highlights from her long adventurous life.

If you would like to leave a review, we appreciate it, and would enjoy knowing how much you liked the book as well.

TL&MR

Chapter One

Amanda's hair whipped about in the cold wind. The pristine blue skies and sunshine were deceptive. The frigid air biting at her cheeks caused the sensitive skin to go numb. Why the hell had she decided to go to an island getaway in the middle of fall? Where did the warmth go? Only last week the temperature soared to near eighty. What she wouldn't give for those temps again.

Around her, the emotional energy nosedived, plummeting to the negatives. She knew some of it belonged to her, but there were others. Amanda glanced over at the kid near the bow of the boat. She spotted him the minute he set foot on the vessel. He had a strange aura about him. Hyper, yet reserved. He carried the burdensome weight of responsibility and failure. His shoulders were rolled slightly forward to protect from the wind, but also, she had a feeling, to shield him from whatever demons he waged war against.

Tall, with sandy-blond hair, he had a geeky quality to him. She grinned. Probably loved video games or something equally as nerdish. *Coffee,*

Amanda, is always a good ice breaker. She crossed the walkway and waited in line. Again she glanced over at the boy on the bow. *Better go with hot chocolate.* Grabbing herself a cup of coffee, she picked up a hot chocolate for the kid then made her way over to him.

The military psychologist she saw on a regular basis would say she was deflecting her own recovery by focusing on someone else in need. Perhaps. But she hated feeling the conflicted emotions racing through him. In fact, he'd been the first person to get under her walls since she closed herself off to everyone. He intrigued her.

"You looked like you could use this," she said, handing over the cup. He glanced at her and cocked a brow. He didn't take it right away, instead studying her with intense hazel-blue eyes.

"Thanks," he replied.

A man of few words. Interesting. She tucked an errant strand of her hair behind her ear and watched as a bank of fog grew closer. It seemed to separate them from something. The island? She didn't know, but it seemed out of place.

"So, the weather huh? Freaky." A weak attempt at conversation on his part, but it would have to do.

She chuckled. "It's nice."

The guy cocked his brow. "You're joking right?"

"Nope. Might be freezing your balls off, but at least you know you're alive." She leaned against the railing. "Why are you going to the island?"

"Downtime." He glanced at the contents of the cup and blew on the hot brew prior to taking another sip. For long moments neither one of them said anything. Then, he cut his gaze toward her, catching her staring at him. "Problem?"

She shook her head. "You don't look like a guy who'd need downtime. What kind of a job do you have?"

"Does it matter?"

"Just curious," she said, holding up her hand. "I thought you could use the company."

"Yeah, sorry. I'm not good company."

The wall of fog she'd spotted on the horizon grew closer. In the next second, they were through it, and the island greeted them on the other side. "You don't say." Holding out her hand, she canted her head when he didn't take it. "I'm Amanda Cutler."

"Patrick."

She lowered her hand and sighed. "You know they can't teach you any social skills on the island."

"Don't want them to." He grunted.

"Amanda," Ben called out, "are you bothering people again?" Her best friend and commanding officer strolled over to them. The man puffed out his chest as he grew closer. Ben carried himself as though he was the baddest mother fucker on the planet and could back up his assertion. She loved him like a brother, and he'd been part of the reason she'd boarded the boat to begin with.

"I'm being friendly." She shrugged. "Can't fault me for trying."

Ben shook his head. "It's obvious the guy doesn't want a shoulder to cry on right now." He stopped next to Patrick. "Name's Ben. Benjamin Kogan."

Patrick snorted. "Well, Ben, Benjamin Kogan, it's good to meet you."

"You're a spook, aren't you?" Ben pitched his voice low.

Amanda scrunched up her nose. "Rude much?" Her friend shrugged. "Look, the kid doesn't want to talk shop." She wouldn't tell him she had already tried to get Patrick to open up.

"I'm just a guy in need of a vacation."

Yeah, she didn't believe his answer. A civilian didn't stand like he was spring-loaded, ready to fight if push came to shove. He was something. Whether or not he'd admit to it, she didn't know.

"Uh huh," Ben said, elbowing him. "I'm in the trade. I know how this goes."

"How what goes?"

"You say you're not. We both know you are." He glanced out over the bow of the boat. "It's a game."

"So," Patrick stated, clearly not interested in continuing Ben's little *game*. "What are you going to the island for?"

Her friend gave him a devastating smile, meant to melt any girl's panties. She'd witnessed his prowess over the years. "I've got a date."

"Really?"

She rolled her eyes. "He hopes he does. If the girl was smart, she'd run the other way."

Ben gave a nonchalant shrug. "She won't be able to resist my charms."

Amanda laughed.

Patrick walked away from the railing, leaving Ben and Amanda to watch the boat ease toward the dock. "You sure about this?" Ben seemed convinced his future waited on the island. He'd practically said as much when they had spoken about it the other day.

"Yup."

He rested his elbows on the wood railing, slouching a bit. It took some of the weight and pressure off his injured knee—a knee she'd contributed to hurting. A wave of guilt washed over her. If she'd only had the courage to suck up her fears for even five seconds and told him the truth.... "How can you be so damn sure?"

"Do we have to go over this again?" Ben's clipped tone warned Amanda to back off. Too bad she didn't know when to say when.

"Maybe." She smirked, raising the cup to her lips for another sip.

"And maybe, once we get on the island, I'm going to have to make you do some PT." Ben glanced at her over his shoulder. Amanda stuck her tongue out at him, and he grinned.

"I'm on vacation," she quipped.

"Till the boat docks. Then, you're back under my command. And Rekkus'."

She gave an unladylike snort. She didn't fear Ben. Rekkus, on the other hand...an argument could be made for him. Amanda didn't miss the smirk on her friend's face. "I'm not sure which one of you is worse."

"Me," Ben replied as the boat bumped into the dock. "Go get your shit and get settled. We'll meet later to discuss what we'll be doing this week."

"Aye, aye, Commander."

"Smart ass," Ben mumbled as he turned and grabbed his gear before disembarking.

It didn't surprise her when he left the boat first. He made a habit of it. It had also saved his life more times than she wanted to count. No matter if a place was considered *safe,* his training dictated he check it out for himself.

Amanda stepped onto the dock with her bag in tow, and, with a head bob in Ben's direction, headed off toward the Haus.

It seemed cooler here than on the boat. It

surprised her. The sun beat down on her, hardly cutting the bitter air as she pulled the door open to step into the lobby. A couple of people milled around the warm and inviting space. Amanda continued past the plush couches and chairs to the woman who sat behind the front desk. The woman's delightful aura complemented her spunky pixie haircut and purple highlights.

"Welcome to Wiccan Haus, Amanda. I'm Myron." A deck of cards sat in front of her, waiting to be used.

"Hello," Amanda replied, not at all surprised Myron knew her name. Unlike the human guests, she knew about paras and how they existed in the world. It had been part of her Para Elite training. "Erm, your name tag says Cammie."

The woman glanced down then blew out a breath. "Some days I feel as though I'd lose my head if it weren't attached." She laughed then clicked a few keys on her computer. "We have you set up in one of our cabins," Myron stated, reaching for the key on the hook. "Cabin three, to be exact."

"Yeah, that isn't going to work." She'd been sent there to train, not squirreled away like some frightened girl.

Myron ignored her, placed the keys in front of Amanda, and began to lay out cards into a simple pattern. "Of course it is. It's a beautiful cabin. Spacious, serene, and secluded." Myron glanced up. "Just what the doctor ordered."

Amanda fought to keep her expression neutral at Myron's odd comment about the doctor. Were the Rowans aware she had closed herself down? The military psychologist had assured her on numerous occasions everything she said would be kept confidential. But one never knew. Ben didn't even know the extent of what she could do or see. He'd freak out if he did.

"I'm here for some additional training with Rekkus and my commander. I require a room at the main house."

"Rekkus is the one who requested you stay in a cabin," Myron said, studying the cards spread out in front of her.

Shit. No amount of hemming and hawing would change the woman's mind, not to mention Rekkus'.

"Okay. Whatever." Amanda sighed in frustration, snatching the cabin keys in front of her. "Can you let Ben Kogan know where I am?"

"Rekkus will inform him," Myron replied, a wide smile curving her lips. "Wow, you're in for an amazing week."

"Sorry?"

"No need to be sorry. I'm kind of jealous. Lucky girl." Myron pressed a button on the counter and a young man appeared at the desk almost immediately. "Please show Miss Cutler to her cabin. Let us know if you need anything, dear. We're always willing to assist."

The bellhop reached for her bag at the same moment she slung the strap over her shoulder. "I got it. Thanks."

"You know, you really need to stop that. It's okay to ask and receive help from time to time. No one thinks less of you," Myron stated in a gentle tone.

"Habit," Amanda replied. "And they are extremely hard to break." She followed the bellhop out of the lobby to the waiting golf cart.

"This way, miss," he said, taking her bag and loading it in the back. "Did you have a good trip in?"

His cheerful disposition banished her uneasiness. "I did, thank you." She got into the cart beside him. "So, do you enjoy your job here?"

His happiness spiked. "Yes. I like serving others. It makes me feel—"

"Warm?" she answered for him.

"Oh yes. My name is Isaac." He drove away from the main building.

"It's good to meet you, Isaac. Where are we going?" The soft rolling hills along with the meadows had a peacefulness about them she craved. To her right, leaves from the orchard trees floated to the ground in a gentle breeze. Apples clung to the branches, ready to be picked, while fall wildflowers bloomed, delighting in the crisp autumn air. Tomorrow, she promised herself, she'd explore the island.

"We have a special cabin for you. It's tranquil, so it will help you quiet your senses and heal. Plus, it's on the water. How can you say no to that?" He followed the main path then took the left leg of the Y. "There is only one other couple using these cabins. They'll arrive later today."

"Swell," she said. "Just me and the water."

"And the other couple," Isaac reminded her.

The rolling hills gave way to soft beaches and gorgeous cabins. Amanda sucked in a breath. The small A-frame cabins had glass walls and thatched roofs. A curving staircase would take whoever stayed there right to the water's edge. If it'd been warmer, she'd have taken a dip or five during her little vacation. However, it didn't mean she couldn't sit on the small balcony and watch the sunset or the stars travel across the sky.

"Wow," she said in a breathless tone. "It's

absolutely beautiful."

"I have to remind you, Serena likes to swim at all hours of the day and night."

"Oh," Amanda replied. "Okay."

"She's our resident mermaid."

"Makes sense now." She laughed. "I'll remember. Anything else?"

"Dinner is at six," he stated, pulling the cart to the staircase. "You are required to attend." He got out, and she followed. "If you need anything, there is a phone in your room. Call Myron. I also have to tell you; you can't make calls out. We're remote out here and your primary concern while you're with us is to heal. Can't do it if you're calling home all the time."

True. "Thanks." Amanda climbed the stairs to her cabin and waited as Isaac opened the door for her.

"I'm not sure if you saw it, but there is a shack located at the end of the dock. Inside you'll find three carts. If you'd rather ride than walk, you're welcome to it." He placed the key on the small table next to the door. "Have a good evening, Miss Cutler."

"Thank you, Isaac. You, too." The man grinned again and happiness spread through her. "How long a walk is it back to the main building?"

"Thirty minutes. Hence, the golf carts." He winked.

Amanda laughed. "Of course."

The door clicked behind Isaac. The spacious cabin blew her away. Everything had been done in natural-colored wood, from the exposed ceiling to the hardwood floor under her feet. A canopied bed sat catty-cornered facing the ocean. Cream-colored gauze curtained the bed.

On the dresser sat a basket of fresh fruit and

nuts. She had a sneaking suspicion everything in the bowl had been grown on the island. She pushed the sliding glass door open then stepped out into the gentle breeze. Amanda closed her eyes and breathed in the fresh air. She could get used to this.

She glanced over at the empty cabins on either side of her and wondered who the other couple was joining her. Wiccan Haus helped everyone. If they were coming out to the cabin, they'd have to be like her, right? In Para Elite, there were others like her and then some. Shifters were a big surprise, but the ones she met were amazing, if stubborn. A blonde wearing almost nothing surfaced in the lagoon and waved. "Hi."

"Hello," Amanda replied. "Aren't you cold?"

"Not at all." The woman laughed. "The water is fine. Beautiful, actually. I'm Serena."

She figured as much. "Amanda," she answered.

"It's good to meet you. If you ever want to talk, come sit by the edge. I'll find you."

"Okay." She grinned. "Thanks."

"You're welcome." The mermaid dove then came back up. "I almost forgot. There is a porthole in the floor of your living area. If you, you know, do anything, you might want to make sure it's not over the glass floor."

"Oh I'm not. I mean...." She cleared her throat. "You have nothing to worry about. I won't be doing anything like *that* while here."

Serena shrugged. "Suit yourself. I'll see you around, Amanda."

"Yeah, see you." The mermaid disappeared again. "Strange freaking place."

Chapter Two

333 BCE
Euphrates River

The trap was set. For so long, she'd struggled under the rule of Darius the III. Their rotten families did nothing but use her gift for ill. Of course, so did her parents. In the beginning, they'd used her stories as ways of gaining what they wanted. Her father yearned for the shepherd's land to graze his paltry, malnourished sheep. Her mother desired only the finest of silks to wear, so she sought to take the tent of a merchant—by force if need be. Her parents conspired day and night, devising schemes of foolhardy nature.

Nai talked in her sleep occasionally. Her ramblings, though not meaningful to her at the time, held a wealth of information her parents could take advantage of. They wrote down everything and, after several days of planning, they went to Darius the III himself, to tell him of the treachery befallen the beauteous city of Pasargadae. Enraged by the plots to overthrow him, Darius the III pulled the shepherd from his land, and the merchant from his stall, and threw them into the putrid cells of the capital. Two days later, their heads were severed from their bodies as a reminder to everyone who challenged Darius the III rule.

When Nai learned her sleep-addled babbling had helped kill those who had the audacity to have more than her parents, she refused to help them or the king in any endeavor, instead choosing a more solitary life.

Unfortunately, being an oracle had its limits. She never knew what would come of her life, only the lives of those around her. If she happened to be have a personal connection to them, she sometimes received glimpses of her future entwined with theirs.

Five summers came and went and during that time, she learned to control her visions. Honing them to the point where she could rest without fear of spilling someone's future.

She was fifteen when Darius the III's men appeared at her hut, took turns raping her until they each had their fill then brought her battered body to the king. His cold, venomous words rang clear in her head. "A pity an oracle such as you would resist the finer things in life. A gilded cage is where you'll stay until such time I see fit to release you on my prey." Later she found out, through slaves and concubines, her parents sold her to the king.

Her enslavement had brought her parents two goats and a chicken, plus the envy of those who conspired with them....

The years passed with little to no change in her status. If she had thought to escape, all those she considered friends died horrible deaths in front of her. Since she'd refused to voluntarily help, she never saw their deaths and, in turn, shame and guilt weighed heavily on her soul, leaving behind a black stain she'd never remove.

Two more years passed. Deep sadness settled over her like a dark cloud promising flooding rains. "Ah, there you are," Darius the III said, a brilliant smile spread across his lips. "It is time to fly, my beautiful bird." He clapped his hands twice and a harem of women descended on him. "Tonight, you will greet the great Alexander, and you will destroy him."

"How?"

His smile never faltered as he spoke. "By feeding him misinformation, of course." His gaze slid over her and revulsion slithered down her spine as he brushed his knuckles against her cheek. "I have spread many rumors of your powers and your beauty. We both know Alexander can't refuse a willing, tantalizing woman." Darius' arrogance knew no bounds. "When he sees the great oracle has gone free, he will take you for his own. Then I will use his ego to crush him and those who dared to fight by Alexander's side."

She lifted her chin in defiance. "And if I don't?"

He snapped his fingers. A woman appeared, carrying the infant she'd given birth to no more than three months prior. "I will kill your daughter."

No. Though she'd been blind to the life expectancy of her child, she also couldn't allow him to kill her. This was her one chance to free herself and her daughter. "Fine. When I have done this task, you will release my child. Send her away."

He fisted her hair and gave her a shake. "This is not a negotiation. Go. Now. Spread your legs for the mighty Alexander the Great. If you are successful, you'll live another day."

Desert winds whipped around her. The sandstorm had forced Alexander's men to take shelter behind the dunes. The day had finally come to watch those who ruthlessly used her die slow, torturous deaths. After spending years locked in a cage overlooking the city she once considered home—while being beaten daily if she didn't reveal some tidbit of information—she found her freedom. A caged bird no more, she stretched her wings and took comfort from the man in her dreams. Alexander the Great. Alex, to those he cherished. And cherish her, he did.

The man had a fetish for boys and women. She even participated in his dalliances a time or two. He was a skillful lover, bringing her to heights untold. Then he cared for her with the utmost tenderness. She fancied herself half in love with the general. Though her kind of love came through rose-colored glasses and little girl fantasies. And, though she could not call him hers, she stood beside him, taking down those who caused her pain.

Nai relayed to him the plans Darius the III put into motion to destroy their army at Gaugamela and seize control of Macedonia. Revenge, pure and simple, had been on her mind along with saving her baby and she had the perfect plan to subvert Darius' men.

At twilight, a lunar eclipse began. The sky darkened, masking Alexander's men as they advanced. Perched on a sand parapet, she watched as one by one Darius' men fell under the cover of complete darkness. By the end of the eclipse, none of Darius the III's men remained. Their blood soaked the sand and traveled down the Tigris River.

Yes, her version of revenge was sweet and satisfying. However, she never returned to the palace to rescue her daughter. Instead, she had the babe whisked away with Alexander's help.

The orgy that followed the battle was hedonistic. The sharing of male and female flesh, decadent. Writhing with the wave of arousal and sexual energy flowing through the ornate tent in the middle of the desert amplified all of her abilities. They ate and drank from the flesh, while fucking at leisurely paces. She thrived with Alexander. Became a master manipulator with Alexander. Though she saw his death the day she joined him, she'd not change a single minute of their existence together. The lessons she learned, the fears she vanquished, were all due in very large part to him. The last time she left his tent, three weeks before his death, he wished her well. "In this life and the next," she whispered, then took her leave....

Resting her hands on the balcony railing as memories of her long and well-lived life rolled through her mind, Nai sighed. She had never found her daughter and convinced herself over the years it had been for the best. No daughter or son during those tumultuous times, would have survived ,and if they were like her...no, she couldn't dwell on it. From the moment she left Alexander's camp, she put her enslavement behind her and moved forward, evolving through time.

Change again would come to pass, affecting both her and her mate—who happened to be standing behind her at the moment.

"I know you're there, Arcades." Nai used his formal name instead of Cade. Something she rarely did.

"Did you have another vision, *hjarta*?" His deep, slightly Nordic-accented voice drifted from the door, sending shivers of delight through her body. She hoped to catch a glimpse of the woman invading her visions, but to no avail. She remained unsuccessful in spotting the auburn-haired beauty.

She wouldn't tell him how disappointed she'd been or the fact she'd wanted so badly to meet their future mate. His warmth greeted her first as he came up behind her. It never failed to amaze her how her body reacted to her mate. Even now, after almost seventy years together, his intonation alone had the power to excite and entice her in ways no other man or woman ever could.

"Not one of *this* time." Though she'd never tried to lie to him, she didn't believe she could either. Although, she had been known a time or two to leave pertinent pieces of information out. Like now.

"Anything more on the auburn-headed woman?" The air around her shifted when Cade stepped out onto the balcony and took her into his arms.

"No." She relaxed against him. Cade towered over her tiny five foot five frame by more than a foot. Massive in human form, he became even bigger when he shifted to his polar bear. His imposing figure never scared her. Quite the opposite in fact. He always made her feel extremely safe and protected. With her past, the safety and security he provided made her love him even more.

"Your visions are never wrong."

He couldn't be more correct, but because her visions foretold a change in their future it had been blurry, at least the parts having something to do with her. Cade and the auburn-haired woman, well, she had seen them in vivid detail. It was those visions that brought them here to Wiccan Haus for the week.

"No, they are not, but sometimes they also don't give the full picture. Sometimes they require me to decipher them. I do not wish to make a mistake," Nai answered. In the distance a seagull took flight. The edge of its wings skimmed across the water.

"Well, if it means anything, I trust you and I'll always trust your visions." Nai felt the deep growl in his chest as he tightened his arms around her.

"Yet you have questions." She turned her head to gaze up at her mate. Glacier blue eyes meet her head on, never wavering.

"Of course I have questions, *hjarta*. You come to me and inform me you have a vision that will impact our life, and how we must come here."

A wave of guilt rolled through her. When telling Cade her visions, she'd deliberately left out certain things. He thought they were simply here to help this auburn-haired woman, and they would. Yet, she hadn't told him she had seen him and the woman having sex. This was impossible, unless the auburn-haired woman had been a potential second mate.

"It seems to me a piece of the puzzle is missing," he stated. "Is she perhaps a polar bear?"

"No. She is not a shifter. She hides."

"Do you think it's our job to bring her out into the light?" he asked.

"No, she must want to do that on her own, although I believe we will guide her."

"Maybe this isn't the correct time place and time to find her, *hjarta*."

"I have the correct time and place." She stiffened No one questioned her visions. Rulers had decimated countries, killing thousands of men, women, and children to possess her and her visions.

"Of course, my queen," he murmured, nuzzling her neck.

"Then we will leave it at that."

Turning her around, Cade picked her up and lifted her to sit on the marble railing.

"Cade!" Nai snarled. "It's freezing."

"I'll warm you, *hjarta*." He pulled her to the very edge then settled between her thighs. "But only after you have been adequately punished for feeling like I questioned your visions."

"*Cade!*"

"Quiet." He leaned forward and rubbed his nose against hers. "Or I'll pull your skirt up and sit you there naked."

"So what exactly is my punishment?" She pouted, shifting on the uncomfortable marble.

"This," he stated.

"Cold is your thing, mate. Not mine." She groaned when he cupped her aching breast. Sparks of pleasure danced along her flesh as he ran the calloused pad of his thumb over her hard nipple.

"Hence why it's your punishment. No worries, though. I'll promise to do my best to warm you." He growled as he slipped his palm under the silky material of her blouse.

"This is dangerous. I'm close to the edge of the railing. Below us are shallow waters. Wouldn't want me to accidentally fall in and catch my death, would we?" Another moan escaped her as he pinched her nipple between his fingers.

"I won't let anything happen to you. Ever," he proclaimed, pushing her shirt up and out of his way, before leaning down to feast on her exposed breasts. He spoke the truth. Her Psi-Guard took his responsibility to love and protect seriously. He'd never allow injury to befall her. "You are beautiful in the moonlight, *hjarta*. Should I tell you how I plan on mating you in the moonlight?"

"Umm." Nai sighed. Leaning back as much as she could, with his arm around her back, anchoring her to him. "I'd rather you show me." She fit her hands between them and cupped his junk, squeezing it. His harsh curse and snarl of pleasure rocketed through her. Always so unabashedly uninhibited with his arousal, he matched her carnal hunger.

She popped each tab free of his button-fly jeans with care, exposing inch by scintillating inch of his rock hard cock to her perusal. She swiped her thumb through the bead of pre-cum pearling at his crest then lifted it to her mouth to taste him. Hot, masculine spiciness, along with something wild and untamable, exploded on her taste buds. His grunt, coupled with the curl of his lip, turned her on.

Nai wrapped her hand around the thickest part of his shaft, and stroked. She loved the sounds he made. The decadent way he shifted his hips, to push more of his dick into her hold. She knew this man well, knew what the beast liked, and used it to her advantage.

A slight tremor worked through his body, and his eyes closed. "Nai," he whispered. "Gods, woman."

"Who's being punished, my *orm-am?*"

"You." He growled, tugging her forward. Cade pushed her hand out of the way, lined himself up with her entrance then fed his cock into her with one long, slow thrust.

Throwing her head back, she cried out. He stretched her, filled her completely, touching her everywhere. He removed her scarf first and placed it on the chair behind them. Then he took off her silk shirt, exposing her skin to the cold, late fall evening. Her nipples hardened to pinpoints. The slight breeze caressed her overly heated flesh, causing goose bumps to break across her body. He latched onto her nipple, sucking on the tight bead with each shift of her hips.

He fucked her like a possessed, starved man, and perhaps he had been. So consumed with her latest vision of the auburn-haired women destined to upend their lives—for the better—she'd neglected her mate. He switched to her other nipple while slamming his hips against hers at a pounding pace. His finger dug into her skin, adding to the burn of lust flowing though her. The urgency in which he took her stole her breath and her senses. She grabbed onto him, digging her nails into his back while meeting him stroke for stroke.

The knot of desire in her belly expanded. Each thrust took her higher. Nai wrapped her legs around his waist. The point of her kitten heels pressed into his ass, and he went wild. With one arm wrapped around her waist, the other gripped her nape. He lifted her with ease and brought them over to the lounger, where he leaned back. "Ride me, *hjarta*. Make us come."

Nai swiveled her hips. In this position, he filled her to the point of exquisite pain. "Are you ready for this to end so soon?"

Cade grinned. "End? This is just the beginning. Once we're done here, I plan on fucking you in the shower and our bed."

She moaned. The muscles of her pussy quivered as he guided her over him. The pace slowed as he rocked her against him. On each down stroke she added a swivel of her hips. The sensations crashed over her like a giant wave, before shoving her back into the bliss. Her head fell back on her shoulders while her hands caressed her breasts. She teased her nipples, plucking the hard peaks then eased off. Her clit throbbed.

"Cade." She whimpered.

"Tell me, *hjarta.*"

"Touch me. Help me," she sobbed, shuddering as she clamped down on him.

"Where?"

"My clit," she moaned, riding him harder.

"As you wish, my queen." He slid his thumb through her cream before pressing down on the hard nub.

She cried out. Her hips jerked as sparks of pleasure shot through her. "Don't stop. Keep going."

He worked her over his length while playing with the swollen bundle of nerves. Everything coalesced inside of her until all she could concentrate on was the rhythm of their lovemaking and feeling of him being buried deep within her. Cade eased her forward and murmured in her ear. What he said, she didn't know. The words were sweet sounding and in his native tongue, adding to the erotic undercurrents flowing through them. The Nordic dialect thickened, and his voice turned gravelly. A thrill of excitement rolled down her spine.

She tilted her head to the side, exposing the column of her neck. She loved it when he bit her. The added rush of being claimed so completely sent her falling over the edge. Her body tightened around him; her breath hitched. Everything dissolved around her seconds before his teeth latched onto her neck. Nai screamed, fracturing into a million pieces. In those moments, she became one with the universe. Strange and she supposed a bit eccentric, sure, but not so outlandish.

Draped over her mate's chest, she gathered her tattered wits. "Are you sure you have the stamina for a repeat performance?"

His laugh vibrated through her. He retreated then filled her again. "I am if you are."

"So you are," she said with a grin.

He ran his hand down her back in a soothing manner. "Whatever this vision is, we will face it together. Do not withhold anything. I can take it."

She sighed. He could. She, on the other hand.... "We will cross that bridge when we get to it."

"Yes, my queen."

Chapter Three

Feeling restless, Cade slipped from their bed and headed into the attached bathroom to get ready for his day. He didn't have to worry about being quiet, as Nai slept like the dead. From experience he knew she would simply wake when her body deemed she'd had enough rest.

After finishing his shower, he quickly dressed in camo pants and a T-shirt. The cold weather didn't affect him, and often he wore summer clothing all year long. A point that drove Nai crazy, since she seemed to always be cold. Cade grabbed his boots before stopping outside the bedroom to raise the heat for his little mate. She'd wake to a warm, comfortable space.

The cold, misty breeze washed over his skin and got his blood pumping as he stepped outside into pre-dawn darkness. Most people used caffeine to jolt them awake in the morning, but he preferred the cold. Worked every damn time.

Plunking his large frame down on the front steps, he made quick work of putting his boots on then went for a run before joining everyone at the training field. Rekkus had mentioned to him when they came through the portal he would be holding various sessions throughout the week. Never one to turn down the additional exercise, he jumped right on it. Nai would be relatively safe on the island, so he could leave her side for a while.

Bright stars sparkled overhead while at the horizon, pink and purple hues pushed back against the early morning sky. Crashing waves created a melodic tune as he moved down the shadowed path at a steady pace. Noise in the distance told him the personnel of Wiccan Haus were slowly beginning to wake up.

Jogging provided him the time to think, mostly about last night and the odd conversation he had with Nai. Something was definitely up. He knew it, could feel it in his bones. His little mate had a way with words. Of course, anyone as old as Nai would know exactly what to say and how to say it so she hadn't outright lied to him. He knew her too well.

Ever since she had brought up this trip to Wiccan Haus, he'd noticed the change in her disposition. Her violet eyes held a note of uncertainty and hesitation. Nai's standard answer when he questioned her was: *"I cannot foretell my future, orm-am. You know this."* He knew it. Everyone knew the truth about her abilities. It's what made her so valuable to the Syndicate. Yet, he often wondered what about his future. As mates, their lives would be intertwined until they died, but it didn't mean shit couldn't happen.

As the sun pushed higher into the sky, he approached the training field. A mix of humans and paras milled around, waiting for Rekkus to begin.

"Name, please?" a no-nonsense voice asked from

his right side. *How did the little slip of a woman get so close without my realizing it?*

"Arcades Bennett."

The little woman glanced down at her clipboard, scribbled something with her tiny pencil, and then peered back up at him.

"You're in group A." She pointed over her shoulder toward the massive oak tree where several other men waited. "We'll be starting in five minutes. Get to know your team." She moved away.

"Know your team? How the hell can anyone know a team in less the five minutes?" Cade chuffed under his breath, as he walked in the direction the woman pointed in. Polar bears weren't exactly known for being the friendliest, and he often had to work to be civil.

"You must be Arcades," a deep voice stated when he had reached the edge of the tree.

"Cade." He scanned the small unit. Not all the members were male. He focused on a tall, slim female with legs that went on forever and made him imagine nasty, dirty things. *Whoa...what the fuck?*

"Ben. Benjamin Kogan." After a quick handshake, the guy asked, "First time here?"

"Huh?" Cade shook his head, struggling to keep his gaze anywhere but on the ass of the woman. "Sorry, uh yeah. It is. You?"

"Yeah, medical leave."

He nodded. "I've heard about you, I think. Para Elite, right?" Cade asked, even though he already knew the answer. Para Elite forces had a look, an attitude to them. The man before him screamed it.

"Yeah. Let me intro you to the rest of the team. Leaning on the tree is Lach. Beside him is Argyle. The two sitting on the ground are Spike and Makka. Sage and Amanda are stretching."

Cade acknowledged them with a curt nod, except for Amanda, who he gave his full attention to. "Ma'am."

She curled her lip at him. "The name isn't ma'am. Save it for your momma. The name is 2C or Commander Cutler." She gave him a once over then went back to stretching. She bent forward and the perfectly round globes of her ass taunted him.

Cade swallowed a growl. None of this made sense. The rush of lust mixed with the punch of desire made his head spin with each move she made. His dick, well used the night before, stirred to life, pushing against the material covering his groin. *How the fuck is this possible?*

"Shut the fuck up, already. We're not here to gossip. We're here to whip your sorry asses back into shape." Rekkus' booming voice cut through his disturbing wants, drawing his focus, albeit slowly, away from the woman warming up her hammies.

So damn bendable. I wonder if she could do the splits while I plowed her. A snarl tore from his throat. Rekkus and the man named Ben cocked their brows. *Son of a bitch.*

"Issues, bear?"

"None," he snapped. For now, anyway. His body hummed with energy. His focus became more keen and attentive as he listened to the tiger explain their mission for the day.

"Capture the flag. As you can see, you have broken down into teams of eight. One will stand guard over your flag while the rest of you defend it with these." He showed them a streamlined paint gun. "If you're shot, you die. Each team has a specific color ball. For the shot to count, it has to be in the middle of the chest or the middle of the back. No head shots allowed."

Fuck yeah. Simple. They used to play a version of it when he was in the Canadian Armed Forces, formally known as the Royal Canadian Army. It taught the units to work together. Sometimes the courses were challenging. Other times not so much. But when it counted in the trenches, each man on his squad would protect one another. Metaphorically speaking, each member of their team when they were in battle became the "flag." Keeping each other safe. Watching each other's backs.

"In a few minutes, we will release your flag carriers to enter the course. Then you will follow. Each team's flag is a different color. The first team to capture two flags, wins. The minute you lose your flag, the game is over for you. You will have five minutes to discuss with your team who will guard your flag. Begin." Rekkus stepped aside as the woman who'd written down his name brought over a lavender banner for their team.

Cade snorted. "Okay, who wants to babysit?"

"Whoa there, pretty boy," 2C said, placing her hand on his stomach. He grunted as an electrical current shot through him at her touch, her soft gasp the only indication she felt it, too, until an overwhelming warmth flowed through him. His bear ate it up, wrapping itself in the soothing tendrils. An empath? She licked her lips. Her honey-colored eyes dilated as the scent of her arousal swirled around him. It took all of his will power not to grab her by the arm, drag her to a secluded spot, and rut inside her until his balls were empty.

Commander Cutler removed her hand from his belly. She swiped it across her hip then glanced down at her palm. *Yeah, peaches, I felt that shit too.*

"Ben and I run a tight ship."

The husky quality did nothing to quell the desire running through his veins. His bear rose up, pushing against his flesh. It took every ounce of his shredded will power to stand there, let alone squash the urge to shift. "My apologies. I'm a take charge kind of guy."

"I'm sure you are," she muttered, snatching the flag out of his hand.

He leaned in when she brushed his side. "Oh, I am." He pinned her with a glare filled with promise. "I see what I want and I take it."

She gasped. The sound went straight to his already raging erection. The tops of her cheeks flushed, and the pulse at her neck jumped. Good, he liked the idea of her being just as affected as him. The idea also pissed him the hell off. How did a mated bear find a woman he'd had no relations with attractive in the sense of, if-he-didn't-get-inside-her-he'd-die kind of way? He shook off the thought and turned his attention back to the game, even as the niggle at the back of his mind said he was forgetting something important.

"As I was saying," Commander Cutler reiterated. Her stance screamed control and in charge. She spread her legs slightly, bracing herself. Her arms were behind her back and her chest. "Eyes on my face, not my breasts, Bennett."

Fuck, those tits are like two damn melons, waiting to be plucked and devoured. He closed his eyes and mentally berated himself. "Sorry, ma'am." Her scathing gaze said she didn't believe a word he said. Neither did he. He didn't give two shits if she knew he openly eye-fucked all of her six foot tall body. *Amazon goddess for the fucking win.*

28

"Again, without further interruptions." Her snarl did nothing to tamp down his urge to mount her. In fact, it only made it worse. "Argyle, I want you to guard the flag. Spike and Lachlan, I want you to climb the trees, get into position where you can, and stay hidden. The rest of you are with me. We're taking point."

His head snapped in her direction. Had she really said run with her? "Ooorah, Commander."

Cade stayed back in the pack as they moved through the woods with silent purpose. He wanted—no, screw that—he needed to watch Amanda's heart-shaped ass shimmy back and forth as they sought their targets. Her ass was a work of fucking art. So much so he couldn't even concentrate on the object at hand. It didn't help that his dick was so hard it throbbed against his zipper.

This is fucked up. He was fucked up. He and Nai and were mated. She wore his mark. Their souls had bonded. So, what the hell?

"She'll have your balls if you keep up your shit." Ben's soft, somber voice broke through his thoughts.

"And she would have every right to." Cade gritted his teeth as a wave of embarrassment washed over him. This desire...this need for the woman in front of him, dishonored Nai and their mating.

"Sometimes you can't help who you want," Ben stated, his tone knowing.

"As you desire the overly timid woman on Rekkus' team."

Ben's head jerked up.

"I noticed how you couldn't take your eyes off her while we waited. Does she know?" It'd been the only thing he could do to try and pull his attention away from Amanda. If he had it bad for a woman he didn't know, Ben had a hard-on for the woman doing everything in her power to hide in plain sight.

Ben snorted.

"That isn't exactly an answer," he responded, more than happy for the distraction.

"She's been sent here to heal."

"And you hope to be part of her healing?" Cade asked.

Ben nodded. "Shit. Here they come."

Rekkus and Cyrus trotted toward them. "They will protect her at all costs." Cade said.

"That's the thing. She'll never need protection from me."

"What the hell is going on with you two?" Rekkus growled out as reached them. "We expect better from you both, and here we find you at the back of the pack, like two new recruits."

"I'm pacing myself. No point blowing out my knee on the first day," Ben stated.

"And what about you, Cade? What is your reasoning for bringing up the rear?" Cyrus asked.

Fucking retrocogger know-it-all. The guy had a bad habit of prodding where he didn't have any business. He tended to give Cyrus a wide berth whenever they were around each other—which he made a point of being hardly ever.

"Does it have anything to do with those pent-up...emotions?" He shook his head. "You're an asshole for this. How do you think Naimh will react?"

Mother fucker.

"Who's Naimh?" Ben asked.

"His mate," Rekkus eagerly replied.

"Fuck." Ben turned to glare at him.

"Nai will be aware. I can't hide anything from her anyway." Cade shrugged.

"If you say so, bear."

"I do." He grunted, raising his gun toward his shoulder. "Now, if you don't mind." He pushed past both men who stared at him like he'd done something wrong. "Poking your nose in where it doesn't belong could get you shot." He grinned to himself while picking up his pace.

Before he got out of arm's reach of Rekkus, the man's giant paw landed on his shoulder. "Tread carefully, bear. I'd hate to have to explain to your bonded why I took a chunk out of your ass."

Cade heard the undercurrent of power in Rekkus' voice. "My bonded loves my ass too much."

"Then let's hope it stays intact."

With a curt nod, Cade continued on. The warning, though said in an even tone, had gotten through to him loud and clear. Don't fuck with the tiger or his charge.

Ben caught up with him seconds later, a look of disbelief still on his face. "I can't believe you threatened to shoot them."

Cade shrugged. "Eh, it's not like they wouldn't do the same to us, given the circumstances. They weren't about to jack their jaws for the hell of it. Right now, friendships don't matter. If they're on the other team, they're the enemy." He tramped through the forest, catching up to Amanda, who'd crouched behind a fallen log. He followed the line of her leg, up to the curve of her ass. *Stop looking at her like she's a piece of meat.*

He couldn't though. Every bit of him wanted her. After approaching her on silent footfalls, he bent down next to her. "What's the situation here?"

"We've got the target in our sights. They're keeping their whole team in front of the flag tower," she said, constantly glancing around.

Ben winced and grabbed his knee as he went down. "I hate this fucking shit."

"Quit bitching," Cade snapped. "You can ice it later, or better yet, get the sweet little bit, Molly, to rub it and make it feel better after we win."

"You're a dick," Ben muttered.

"You're just now figuring this out?" He laughed. "Gotta put your big girl panties on when you're with me."

2C snickered. "Well, if you're such a badass. Clear me a line." She practically threw him out into the clearing. Her deceptive size and loose uniform hid a muscular physique.

Cade used his exceptional hearing to listen for the other team as he crept through the thicket. In front of him, he knew there were players for the opposite team. To the right a bush rustled, and he pulled the trigger. A yelp of surprise followed the splat of the paintball. A woman whose name he hadn't caught headed off the playing field. When she was clear, he continued on, taking his time, picking off player after player. He took another step and felt the crack of a paintball hitting his back plate. "Son of a bitch."

The only good thing about getting hit was Commander Cutler knowing where the asshole hid. He exited the field and watched as four of them advanced, moving through the wooded floor. When they got to where he'd been shot, 2C took aim and fired. The damn panther, Cortez, tumbled from the tree to land on his feet, laughing. The intensity of the game built around them as they cleared the area. With four down, there were at least seven left.

"Watch your six," Commander Cutler called out

to Ben.

The man slowed his pace. The whistled blew, and Tabby came through the middle of the field, carrying a yellow flag. How the hell had she done it? Cortez shrugged. The girl grinned then whooped with excitement. She waved the flag back and forth. Cade trotted out onto the playing field, stopping beside 2C and Tabby. "How did you do that?"

"I have my ways," she said. "No one said we couldn't use our attributes."

Cade shook his head. "Thanks for the game everyone. 2C." He nodded at her. "Congrats." He needed to get away. Run. Do something before he did the unimaginable. Maybe he'd clear his head with a dip in the ocean then go find his mate and fuck whatever this was out of his system. At least then he wouldn't feel as bad as he did at the moment.

Chapter Four

Amanda sat down at a table in the dining hall and groaned. She needed something cold to drink and to see something naked. Since the second didn't appear to be happening any time soon, she'd make do with the shitty stuff Sage said was green tea and eat her vegetarian whatever-the-hell-it-is—getting back to nature, blah. The way-too-energetic herbalist said something about her chakras being out of whack and needing a "detox" diet. What she needed was a twelve ounce porterhouse, medium rare, a huge ass loaded baked potato, and a beer.

She pushed the vegan, or was it vegetarian, concoction—she didn't know what to call it—around on her plate and frowned. What the hell was this place? One minute she thought she had reenlisted in the army and had to do basic again, and the next she thought she entered some hippie commune. How would any of this help her break the chains of her self-imprisonment? *Well, you could start a riot. Attica. Attica. Attica.* A vision of her throwing her tray to the floor and stepping onto her table to protest the inhumane conditions of vegetarian food had her grinning.

Taking a bite of the mystery cuisine, she curled her lip. Ever since she'd touched the polar bear, Arcades, she felt addled. Out of control. Snippets of images rushed through her mind. Him looming over a vision of a woman dressed in fine silks. Fucking her like a bull in rut. The woman's large, violet, almond-shaped eyes—which should have seemed inhuman—accentuated her fine-boned features. The woman's bow-shaped lips parted in pleasure. The eroticism of the scene left her feeling gut punched. Amanda's clit tingled. Her breath hitched. The images had been fresh in her mind as they traveled farther into the forest and almost cost her the game a time or two.

Fucking men, always thinking about sex. Like she was the exception to the rule. If men thought about getting their dick wet every five seconds, her competitive streak demanded she do one better.

"Excuse me," a woman said, her slightly accented voice surprised Amanda, knocking her out of her thoughts. "May I sit with you?"

She glanced up at the woman and her heart stopped. Her brain forgot how to function. The image of the woman laid out in the sun, Cade fucking her, filled her mind once more. "Uh...." A prick of anxiety raced through her. The energy coming from the woman standing before her could make most cower in fear; she, on the other hand, wanted to roll in it. She'd never felt anything like it before. Add to the fact it had been old, not like old lady, moth ball old, but like ancient civilization old. If Amanda had to pinpoint a time in history she'd have guessed the days of the pharaohs maybe? The bright whiteness of her soul called to her. It sang to Amanda. *Amazing.* "Sure," she said, when she finally found her voice.

"Thank you," the woman said. Her almost childlike fingers gripped her burnt-gold cowl and pushed it back, uncovering her head and face. "It's not often I eat alone, anymore."

Amanda gaped at her. Her long, dark-brown hair had been pulled back into a low bun, while two braids were drawn back at her temples and wrapped around the intricate knot at the base of her neck. Those beautiful, large, violet eyes of hers watched Amanda, preternaturally so. The woman from her visions. How in the world. "I...well, I...."

The woman laughed. "It's a pleasure to finally meet you, Commander Amanda Cutler, Para Elite. I am Naimh Laleh, oracle."

Her breath left her in a rush. Oracle. She'd thought they were only fairy tales. "Wow," she said. "I didn't think.... Hi."

Naimh laughed. Even her laughter had sparks of energy in it. Amanda felt instantly drawn to her, almost drugged by the connection forming between them. "Well, as you can see, I am real," she said. "Since I am the first of my kind you've met, how about a story?"

Cutler scrunched her nose up. A story? Why would she want to hear a story? Yet, saying no to this ethereal woman sitting beside her felt disrespectful. She also worried if the woman left her, she'd wither away and die. Strange as it sounded, she couldn't make heads or tails of the tidal wave of emotions surging through her. "Sure, why not. Not like I don't have tons of time on my hands."

After the paintball game, Ben had found Molly in the crowd of competitors while Cade ran off. The other men and women in her unit seemed to pair off as well, leaving her alone. It didn't bother her, though. She'd spent many nights in distant places on para missions by herself. But the island had a weird way of making you crave the things you never knew you wanted. Like a partner and stability and a life.

Naimh leaned in close. "What do you know of the pirate Anne Bonney and her partner, Mary Read?"

Amanda smiled. "Anne Bonney was a take-no-prisoner, badass bitch." She cleared her throat. "Pardon my language."

Naimh gave a throaty laugh. "Ah, so she was. While you eat, I'll tell you a story about the time I met the pirate, Anne."

For some inexplicable reason, she wanted to eat the bland food on her plate, just so Naimh would continue to talk. If anyone else had come to her and said the same as her new oracle friend, she'd have pushed them aside, called them delusional, and more than likely left. Not with this oracle, though. She was legit.

"The year was 1720, and the beaches of Nassau were rich for the taking...."

***

"Jack, if I've told you once, I've told you a thousand times—this island will eat you alive." Anne's husky voice cut through the whipping wind of the ocean.

"Darling," he replied. "It's full of money ripe for the pillaging. We entertain ourselves here, wait for someone to pass out, and take what they've left." He cozied up to Anne. His lips brushed the shell of her ear. "We'll fuck under the stars while drinking rum."

Anne rolled her shoulders. "We'll get shot is what we'll do."

Jack's hand splayed across Bonney's stomach. "I'm sure Mary will join us, won't you, dear?"

She licked her lips. Anne had been a veracious lover. The way the woman ate pussy could be considered, although crudely, an art form. The first time she laid with her, Bonney spread Mary's legs wide then settled between them and drank of her flesh. The orgasms were amazing, the little tricks she learned far more important. "I will," she said. "I have seen what debauchery lies before us."

It had been her suggestion to join with Jack that led them toward the Bahamas and now Nassau Beach. Merchant ships were anchored a few miles from shore, filled with precious booty, which would be used for trade. Ransacked man-o'-war ships were also being prepped for battle, claimed by the pirates who'd made the island their home.

"Vane is also here," Anne reminded him.

"It will be fine," Jack answered. "The cur lost his nerve years ago. Not like we didn't send him on his way. Right, men?" he called out.

The rousing "Aye" that followed did nothing to sooth her fears.

They'd talked the night before, after a stimulating round of lovemaking. Jack was a reckless man, sometimes picking fights with those he knew couldn't win. She ran her fingers through Bonney's hair, whispering words of encouragement, knowing their time was coming to a close. Three years together had seemed like centuries. She loved Anne with all her heart. So, she made the best of what remained of their life together.

"Anne," she said, coming up beside her. "We'll have fun. Find a whore or three to play with. Jack can join in." She gave him a teasing look. "If his

prick will rise."

That got a laugh out of her friend. "I suppose you're right," she said. "Three days, Jack."

"Of course, darling."

Three days turned into a month. A month turned into six. Nassau became a port of refuge for them. Due to her abilities and Anne's cunning, they'd taken over the whorehouse. They'd put the old woman running it out of her misery and turned it into a booming business. Even if it meant gutting a man to get their point across.

No one stole from Anne Bonney and Mary Read, as she called herself in those days.

Pirates from all over diverged on that beach. Blackbeard. Long John Silver. Billy Bones. Each had been more delectable than the last. Each one told her secrets by candlelight. A few times she'd been tempted to follow them, leave the island behind, and create a new adventure for herself, but she stayed with Anne.

In the summer of 1720, they finally left port. Jack had acquired three ships and owned a rather prosperous packing and parcel company. Money flowed to them, hand over fist. A pirate's treasure to be sure. But the call of the ocean drew them from land and sent them back to sea. The night before they departed, she tried to warn Anne and Jack, about the coming raids but neither would listen to her.

For months they rode the waves. Until they got word something big would be happening near Point Negril, Jamaica, and Jack had to be there.

The weasel. Instead of fighting when they were ambushed by the British Armada, he cowered like a little baby in the hull, leaving her and Anne to fend for themselves.

She fought like a feral woman, ready to take out any and all who tried to board their ship. Anne and she stood shoulder to shoulder, swords raised, pistols at the ready. A single shot might not do much, but it would do if one man went down. Completely surrounded, they did not back down.

Together they made as much noise as possible, giving the illusion of a hearty crew behind them, waiting for battle. She knew they'd never make it out of there. When Captain Jack Barnet's men came aboard, she and Anne attacked. They killed three men and injured four more before being overrun and captured. Along with Jack and his drunken bastards, they were shuttled to Jamaica to stand trial.

In the days that followed, Anne realized she carried Jack's child, and in order for them to survive, she played along. Both of them claimed they were with child on the day Jack lost his head along with every member of his crew. The judge asked if they had anything to say, and she explained their delicate situation. Since killing a fetus went against God, they were relegated to their cells.

Days and months rolled together.

Anne used her skills to get them out of jail, calling in all of her favors. When Bonney got them safe passage, there was a catch. Nai had to fake her death. It wasn't hard. They found a woman who looked as she did; only the woman was sick with Spanish flu. They deposited her into the cell then under the cover of darkness, made their escape. Anne helped her get to the French colony, better known as Louisiana, and after wishing her luck, Anne Bonney walked out of her life, forever.

***

Amanda plopped her elbow up on the table and rested her head on her palm when Naimh began to speak. The slight husky tone lulled her into t a trance-like state and Naimh's vivid descriptions told her of what she had lived through. She swore she could feel the wind in her hair, the salt from the ocean on her lips, and the humidity dampening her skin.

"Holy shit." She expelled a breath when Naimh finally finished. "That...you were amazing. I swear I could just listen to you tell story after story."

A twinkling of laughter filled the air. "Part of being an oracle is knowing how to tell a story."

Amanda nodded. "You nailed it."

"Or, as my bodyguard likes to say, I have the gift of gab," Naimh prepared a cup of the green tea for herself.

"May I ask you a personal question?" Amanda asked, not willing to break whatever spell she seemed to be under.

"Of course. Ask away. I am an open book."

"How old are you?"

Naimh lifted her cup to her mouth and took a couple sips before speaking. "I am several millennia old."

"Damn."

"Life has not always been easy for me, but the same could be said for everyone in this world, correct?"

"Yeah, I guess. Although, I think some have had it harder than others," Amanda replied as past memories began to fill her thoughts.

"I have learned to make the best out of what life

has given me. I have lived, loved, and lost a thousand times over and yet here I am." The oracle spread her arms out in front of her and smiled.

"How, though?"

"I have hope." The woman glanced around the room then leaned forward, her voice dropping. "And a passion to live, to explore, and to love." She paused. "Is it not what everyone seeks?"

"To be honest. I think happiness is a fucking illusion."

Naimh clicked her tongue. "Perhaps because you have never allowed yourself to be happy. Or to be free from the bonds that hold you."

Shit! This dainty little woman saw way more than anyone else. Her violet gaze caressed Amanda from head to toe.

"Are you reading me?" A flare of anger rushed through her body at the thought of this woman violating her secrets.

"I have no need to read you, firebrand. It is my profession, remember? I knew exactly who and what you were prior to even sitting down."

Amanda couldn't help the gasp slipping through her lips.

"Do not worry. I will keep your secret, until you proclaim it to the world. When you are ready, of course." She changed the subject. "I'll see you at painting later this afternoon."

Amanda felt like she had whiplash. The oracle went from one tone to the next in the blink of an eye. "What? Sure." She frowned and pushed away from the table. "I have to go." She needed to think and put space between her and this whimsical, enigmatic person who'd so easily captured her attention.

"You desire to hide." Naimh held up her hand as

if to stop any of her protests. "I understand. I do. Believe it or not, I have been in the same predicament as you. You crave embracing who and what you are. Accept it, and you will flourish and find your happiness."

Amanda hurried from dining room. She even rushed past Ben, ignoring him completely.

What the hell was going on with her? This morning after Cade had touched her all she had thought about was fucking him; now her thoughts were the same for the delicate oracle she had left behind in the dining room.

Maybe she just needed to get laid. Yeah, that had to be it. It had to have been at least two to three years since she had a good fucking. Relationships and being in the Para Elite Force didn't go hand to hand. Missions always took priority, and so Amanda only had sex when she needed to scratch an itch. Thankfully, her sexual libido, until today, had seemed to be almost nonexistent.

Fucking figures....

Chapter Five

Nai watched Cade paced the room like a caged bear. A light breeze blew in through the open sliding door. He chuffed and growled while circling the couch where she sat, leaving her a dizzy mess. She wrapped the blanket around her tighter and closed her eyes, unable to stomach his movements any longer.

"Arcades!" she yelled in an attempt to stop his pacing.

"Not now!"

"Oh, I think right now is the perfect time." She patted the empty spot next to her on the couch. "Sit," she commanded, giving him space to plop his ass down. "Now, Arcades."

Cade lumbered over and slumped his hulking frame into the couch next to her. Nai bounced in her seat, a side effect of having such a huge mate.

"I know," Nai assured him laying her hand on his. "You have seen the auburn-haired woman, have you not?" Her bonded would continue to beat himself up, like he was at the moment, for his reaction to Amanda.

"I don't want to discuss this."

"Well, that is too bad, because I do." Determination filled her. "I met her also. Her name is Amanda."

"Nai...."

"It's okay, my love."

"It's not okay. I felt things for her. Wanted to do things to her." His self-recrimination it broke her heart.

"As did I," she stated nonchalantly, ignoring his shocked look. "I told her of my time with Anne Bonney and Jack."

"Seriously? What possessed you?"

"It seemed to fit the mood." She grinned.

"Tell me you left out the part about being lovers with both Jack and Anne?"

"Why ever in the world would I not tell her? It's the juiciest part of the whole tale." She laughed. "It gave her something to think on." *Better for him to seek the truth of his own fruition, than to be given a trail of bread crumbs to follow.*

"Nai." Guilt filled his tone.

"No." She gazed into her bonded's Arctic-blue eyes. *My poor mate. Such sadness shouldn't fill your soul.* "It is a happy time. I promise. Have faith and patience in me."

"Always, *hjarta.*"

He didn't mean it. She could sense his confusion, his anger, and his lust. This was how it had to play out. Amanda needed to free herself in order to live what would become her destiny. Their future together, or as a couple, could still change if Amanda did not choose the correct path.

"I have a date to meet with her later. We are going to paint and I believe I just might tell her about my time with da Vinci next." A slow sensual smile crossed her lips. "It might be a good idea for you to also make arrangements to spend some time with her. Without me."

"Do you know what you're asking of me? What I'm feeling...for her? Do you know what could happen? We're bonded," Cade snapped out.

"If it is fated to happen, then it must." Nai stood and slowly folded the blanket that had covered her before she placed it back on the back of the couch. "Our bond is strong and true."

He stood. His six-foot-eight frame towered over her. He'd never hurt her, could never hurt her. Yet, it didn't stop him from trying to intimidate her occasionally. However, she'd gone head to head with Genghis Khan, William the Conqueror, Edward Longshanks, and Elizabeth the First, to name a few. Nothing intimidated her.

"Tell me what you see," he demanded.

"I cannot. Stop asking." Backing away from him, she started down the hallway. "I'm going to go change since I cannot paint in this outfit." Stepping into their bedroom, she heard his loud chuff. Her poor bonded. If everything went as planned, he'd have to deal with two very headstrong women.

After changing into a long black skirt and free-flowing black top, she left her hair up and applied another coat of her dark-purple lipstick.

"I am off for now," Nai said, pulling the heavy shawl off the back of the chair in the living room. "Please find something to do so you do not drive yourself insane."

Cade growled in response.

"Very well then, be your normal polar bear self."

He reached out to pull Nai into his warm

embrace. "Be careful, *hjarta.*"

"I do not have to be careful; it's why I have you around." She smirked.

"I love you," he whispered as he bent to rub his nose up and down the bridge of hers.

"As I love you," she replied before stepping out of his arms.

She took the long way back to the main part of Wiccan Haus, deciding to walk there instead of drive. Cade needed time to reconcile his emotions. Work through the guilt of finding another betrothed. Another mate to bond them together. Little did he understand, Amanda experienced the same conflict.

The sun hung low on the horizon, and a bear half the size of her mate waded into the water, followed by a completely naked man. Nai grinned. Bonded. Newly so, and like all married couples, testing their adventurous streak.

Stopping for a moment, she watched them splash and bounce in the water before the small bear shifted in a flash of simmering light and jumped into the arms of the man. Ah, young love. They'd experience the same soon. When they convinced their empath to join them.

Following the path, she walked inside the lobby and greeted Myron. "Good afternoon, Myron," she said. "How do you fair today?"

The psychic receptionist nodded. "Very well, Naimh." She continued on her way to class, trying to figure out the best plan of attack. However, when one cannot see what the future holds for themselves, no one could form a plan to follow. She stepped into the classroom and sat down on the stool near the middle of the room. She could feel the anxious energy of her mate as he prowled around outside. She laughed to herself. "Silly old bear."

She'd known he'd trail after her. From the way he paced near the orchard tree line, he fought a losing battle with himself.

The door opened a second later and Amanda stepped inside. She'd never tell Cade this, but she'd worried the girl would hide from them. Looked like she'd been made of sterner stuff than she appeared. "You made it," she said, unable to keep the happiness out of her voice.

"I thought about cancelling," Amanda admitted.

"What stopped you?" Nai asked.

She shrugged. "I don't know."

A better answer than none. "Well, I am glad you decided to come."

Their instructor walked in a few moments later, followed by the same girl Nai had seen bounding through the water only minutes ago. The man who'd been with her took his position at the back of the class while the young girl stood up on the stage.

"Good evening." Sunny, the painting instructor said grabbed her smock then put it on. The pixie glided across the room, her skin shimmering under the illuminating skylights. Only standing about four foot eleven, her presence seemed larger than life. When she turned to the class, her blue eyes sparkled. She made quick work of tying back her long, curly blonde hair before clasping her hands together. "I have a special treat for you today. This is Roxy Harlow-Baxter. She will be your model for the afternoon."

The little bear with the side of her head shaved and the rest of her hair in long curls and small braids removed her robe. From behind them, a chuff of appreciation emerged from her bonded's chest.

"Well, someone is getting a good show. Reminds me of da Vinci."

"You knew da Vinci?" Disbelief filled Amanda's words.

Nai laughed. "I've lived a wonderfully full life. Roxy reminds me of the Mona Lisa."

"What? She looks nothing like the painting."

"What you see in the painting isn't the woman who sat for my friend that day." She leaned in and whispered, "It was two women."

Amanda shivered.

Through the thin material of her shirt, Nai watched her nipples tighten into hard pinpoints. Her mouth watered.

"No way," Amanda breathed, her lips mere inches from Nai. The urge to close the distance became all consuming.

"Yes," she said. The tip of her tongue flicked at Amanda's bottom lip. The startled gasp made Nai's pussy clench. She sat back slowly. "The woman who sat for him first had a, what is the term, butter face?"

Amanda laughed then covered her mouth. "That's not very nice."

Nai gave a nonchalant lift of her shoulder. "Nevertheless, it's true." She dipped her brush in the black paint. "He took her best features and matched them up with the second model's face."

"Did you have sex with him, too?" Had she detected a hint of jealousy in Amanda's tone?

She shook her head. "Though there have been tales of his sexuality, the man was most definitely gay." She began with Roxy's hair. She loved it. The way it flowed down her back and over her shoulder, softening the harshness of her shaved head.

"Really?" Amanda had also begun, but she chose

49

to start with the floral robe the girl had used as a cover up.

"Mmm," Nai replied. "The man was a glorious exhibitionist. Though I only had the pleasure of seeing him in all of his magnificence once, it truly was a sight to behold." She shivered. "Made a lady such as myself wet."

"You're only saying this to get a rise out of me," Amanda quipped. Sunny gazed in their direction, but her arched brow and pursed lips didn't bother Nai one bit.

"Maybe. Or perhaps I am excited to share my life with you. To tell my tales." She continued to paint the young bear.

"Their heat is explosive," Amanda murmured after a while. "I can feel his need. He craves that girl. I swear, if he gets anymore aroused, he'll fuck her right here. Right now."

Nai smiled. "And this would be a bad thing?"

"They are bonded. I don't think they want others to join in, or watch," she answered, biting the corner of her lip in concentration.

"Who said we wouldn't have our own little adventure." From the corner of her eye, she caught a glimpse of her mate a few feet from the window. He'd stopped pacing and had moved on to active listening. *Finally.*

"But you're bonded. I feel it. Why would you want to play with me?"

Why indeed. "A girl has her needs," she hedged. "Besides, I also know you crave me. You went slick when I licked your lip. You've been aroused since we ate lunch. I figure if you'd like, we could sample each other."

Amanda put the brush down and stared at Nai.

"You're confounding. I don't know whether to take you seriously or if I should roll with your good-natured ribbing."

"Well, then there is only one way to find out if I am being truthful," she said.

"Oh?"

"Say yes," Nai said, cleaning the black paint from her brush.

***

Son of a bitch! Hearing Nai tell Amanda they could sample each other, everything became crystal clear for him. Their conversations over the last several days suddenly started to make sense. Her vagueness. Her refusal to answer his questions directly, mixed with what he'd come to realize it all made perfect sense.

Amanda would become Nai and his third, if she accepted who and what she was to them. This news meant one thing: Nai had been withholding information. He would have to address that with her tonight. She knew better, even if she did it by omission to ease his mind.

He leaned up against the wall, listening as the woman continued to talk. His mate told Amanda another story about Robert the Bruce before he became king, and their tryst. Nai seduced her with those erotic stories she loved to tell.

The guilt he'd carried around began to wash away. She needed 2C as much as he did. Whatever issues Amanda faced, they'd help her with. Cade knew if the woman didn't bond with them, it would destroy his bonded mate.

While he had been hiding from his desires, Nai

had been meeting this head on, and so now he had to do so as well. He had to make some gestures toward the woman, which, he suspected, would confuse her. But Amanda needed to get to know them both.

Patience wasn't something he had an abundance of, but as he waited outside the art room until the class finished, he knew he'd do whatever it took to gain her trust. The door opened moments later and men and women began filtering slowly out of the room. Amanda was nowhere in sight. Long moments later, she stepped through the door. He released a building growl from his throat. Dick throbbing in his jeans, he pushed off the wall and surprised her. Panic flashed in her eyes before she had the chance to close off her emotions.

"If you are looking for Naimh, she went the other way, toward the lobby. Something about having to ask Myron a question."

Cade didn't miss the wobble in Amanda's voice.

Good. I affect her as much as she affects me.

"I'm not here for Nai. I'm here to see you." Cade struggled to control his beast. 2C didn't seem ready to accept their bond or believe it.

"What the fuck is wrong with the two of you?" Amanda spat. "You two are bonded and yet neither of you will leave me alone!"

Before she could get too far away from him, Cade reached out and grabbed her hand. A pulse of desire, not unlike what they'd both felt at the training field, rushed through his body. His already aching dick began to throb with an incessant need. The light perfume of her arousal swirled around him.

Damn, she smelled so sweet. He bet she'd taste even better.

"There is no shame in your desiring us," he

replied.

"Bonded don't do this."

"We both desire you, Amanda."

She snorted in response.

"Nai has lived an extremely long and erotic life."

"That doesn't make it right." Frustration laded her voice.

He heard the panic in her tone and knew he needed to calm her. "She has my permission, as I have hers," he assured her, his tone soft and soothing. Later, they'd fuck together and apart. Jealously didn't happen in bonded relationships—even if the experience was new for all of them.

"Seriously?"

"Why would I lie? You will see Nai again. She will tell you another story, attempting to seduce you with her sweet little voice and her very erotic tale about Caesar." He didn't miss the slight smile floating across her lips. "I won't ever lie to you. I happen to enjoy where my balls are," he teased.

"Caesar?"

"A deprived bastard for sure. He threw massive orgies lasting for days on end. According to Nai, he fucked anything and everything on two legs. You'll need about a six months to hear the whole story. She stayed with him for several years."

"Doesn't it upset you? The fact she speaks so fondly of past lovers."

"Those past lovers made my Nai who and what she is today. I thank them and appreciate them. Nai enjoys sex and actively participates. She is a true free spirit. She doesn't allow anyone to hold her down. Unless that is what she is looking for."

"You both confuse the hell out of me."

"It is not our intent. We are trying to get to know

you as individuals. Then together. Is this something you'd be willing to try?"

"Maybe."

"We'll take that maybe. Have a drink with us at our cabin. Then we'll go to dinner together." He hoped to hell he didn't sound as overeager as he felt.

"Drinks and dinner?"

"Yes."

Silence reigned. Just when he thought she wouldn't say anything, she nodded. "Yes."

"Excellent. Allow me to escort you to our cabin." He held out his hand and swallowed the appreciative groan when she slipped her hand into his.

"What about Naimh?"

"I'm sure she has already at our cabin and is waiting for us," he assured her. He knew Nai would rush back to their cabin to prepare it for their little get-together. Cocktails would be waiting, and the mood would be set.

"Do you wish to walk or take the cart?" Cade asked.

"Walk."

"Then so we shall." Cade pulled her close to his side and guided her to their cabin.

Chapter Six

Music played in the background. The lights were turned down, giving their cabin a soft glow. Amanda stepped inside. Nervous energy knotted her gut, even though a pulse of calm hummed along the edges. Nai had disappeared quicker than she'd liked, which only added to the unease coursing through her. Cade nudged her from behind.

"Are you sure?" She licked her lips. "I could come back tomorrow or something."

Always so sure and confident, her stalwart facade cracked, showing her vulnerability. She never allowed anyone to see her this way, choosing instead to be a bitch—correction, the baddest bitch east of the Pecos.

"Relax," he murmured.

"Says the polar bear," she muttered, stepping farther into the space. The cool air of the bungalow surprised her. "Something wrong with your heater?"

Cade laughed. "I enjoy the cold. Let's you know you're alive."

"So does frostbite, but I like having all my appendages attached to my body." She pulled her coat tighter around her.

A shiver worked through her with his deep rumble of happiness. "Nai would tend to agree with you. I compromise. Our home is filled with blankets."

Amanda rolled her eyes. "Such a chivalrous man."

His arm wrapped around her seconds before he pulled her close. The inferno called Cade enveloped her. "Twelve hundred pounds of pure bear heat," he whispered. "You'll never need a blanket when you're around me."

Touché.

"I'll have to remember that little fact," she said closing her eyes. Below the heat, the unmitigated lust singed her synapses. "Cade." The emotional overload sucked her under while also keeping her rooted in her spot. "I can feel...."

"Good." He growled. "It's about damn time. I'm losing my fucking mind here."

"I lost mine a long time ago." She chuckled. "I can't breathe, though."

The melee of sensations bombarding her hadn't happened in years. Not since she'd been awakened. Her whole life she'd been *sensitive*. At one point, she'd believed what doctors told her mother; she had autism. Of course, the doctor qualified it by saying she was also high functioning and intelligent. Because parents wanted to know their child had a genetic disorder, but had a high IQ. Like that *lessened* the blow.

However, it gave her mother a measure of calm, instead of embarrassment. The bouts of laughter for no reason could be explained away now. The uncontrollable crying—anger so rash and unrelenting it threatened to consume her. When she finally calmed, she could never verbalize what made her so unhinged. Nor could she control it.

At the age of twelve, the precognitive visions began, melding with her sensitive nature. Amanda regressed. The idea of being touched, on top of whatever emotion a person might feel, had the ability to drive her insane. Without many options or alternatives, she'd been taken to a mental hospital. Those were her darkest days. Until she met Ruth. The nurse saw her secluded from the other children, rocking back and forth. How the woman knew she wasn't like them, she'd never know.

The woman had pulled her aside.

For six months, she helped Amanda until the day she could block the emotions of others and the visions. Then Ruth introduced her to the Syndicate. From there, her life became a whirlwind of change. She'd been whisked away from everything she knew and those she called family.

"There you are," Nai said, gliding into the room. "I wondered what took you so long."

"She wanted to walk," Cade teased.

"Walking is excellent. It gets your blood pumping and helps you think." Nai smiled. "Remind me to tell you about the time I walked the Great Wall of China, on a dare. It was a life-changing experience. Such a peaceful and quiet walk, for sure."

Amanda couldn't help but smile when Cade waved his hands behind Nai, while shaking his head.

"Stop it, Arcades. That is not funny." Nai never even looked over her shoulder.

"How'd you know what he was doing?" A bubble of laughter escaped her lips as Cade continued.

"Because I know him," she groused. "He thinks he is funny. He is not." Nai looped her arm through Amanda's and guided her toward the sofa. "Sit. I'll get you a drink."

"So, when did you walk the Great Wall of China? Was it recently?" Amanda asked.

Cade sat next to her on the couch.

"No. I walked it several years after it was completed." Nai placed a couple of ice cubes in a tumbler then picked up a bottle of very expensive vodka to cover the ice.

"Who dared you?" Curiosity killed her.

"Emperor Gaozu. He had all these preconceived notions of what a female should and shouldn't do. He often said females were only good for slaking a man's lust and providing them heirs." She moved over to the couch and handed Amanda her drink.

"In his defense, it was 200 BCE. All men thought the same thing at the time," Cade interjected.

"Pfft. Do not make excuses for the men of this world, or blame the time period. I was there. You were not. Many countries thrived on a matriarchal system. Would you like me to list them?" Nai poured two more glasses before returning to the couch.

"Are you two always like this?" Amanda took a sip of her vodka. Served exactly how she liked it—ice cold with a fruity note and a hint of fire.

"Most days. Do you like your drink?"

Wedged between the two of them, a pulse of need ran right through Amanda's body. It was intense and demanding. Her nipples hardened to the point of pain and her sex went slick. "It's lovely. Thank you." Bringing the ice cold glass to her lips, she sucked the remaining vodka down. The warmth of the alcohol mixed with her desires and a fine sheet of sweat covered her body. *Whoa...downing the whole glass at one time. Not one of my best ideas.*

"Would you like another?" Cade's deep timbre

startled her, even knowing she sat right beside him.

"N-no. One is my limit." Sticking her finger into the glass, she rolled the cubes around hoping that the cold might cool her body down and take her mind off the lust pulsing through her.

Silence filled the room for long moments then she felt Nai's fingers wrapping around her wrist to pull her finger out the glass. Leaning down, while keeping eye contact, she sucked Amanda's finger into her mouth. The warmth of the oracle's tongue against her cold skin had her gasping for breath.

Holy shit. Holy shit. Her clit throbbed and her pussy spasmed as a small climax washed over her. Nai released her finger with a pop.

"You taste sweet."

"She smells even sweeter," Cade growled. Amanda dragged her gaze from Nai's to Cade's. Arctic-blue eyes swirled with desire and need. A quick glance down to his lap showed his dick was rock hard, tenting his pants.

Her mouth opened and closed like a fish out of water and finally, her voice returned. "Ahh...umm, yeah. That shouldn't have happened."

"What happened?" Nai asked. "I was a bad hostess and forgot to provide napkins. I simply provided a service for you. One I hope to extend to you again in the future."

What the fuck? Yeah. She needed to get out of here. Like now. "I think I need to go." Jerking out of her seat, she placed the empty glass on the table.

"But what about dinner?" Cade inquired.

"Another time." She needed to get the hell out of there and go back to her room. Spend a little *me* time with her vibrator.

"Tomorrow?" Nai requested.

"Ahh. Yeah. Sure." By then she'd have orgasmed about a dozen times.

"It is custom to provide a kiss when leaving, from where I come from."

"Okay." Amanda bent down, so they were mere inches apart. Nai's soft, delicate hand crept around the back of Amanda's neck as their lips touched. With the intent to keep it quick and simple, Amanda began to back away. Instead, the oracle held her in place and deepened the kiss.

Cade's body bracketed hers from behind, radiating heat. Nai slipped her tongue through her lips. The first touch of her tongue on Amanda's—orgasmic. Her damn nipples were so hard they ached. As if reading her mind, he reached around to cup her full breasts and ran his thumb over the turgid buds.

To succumb to this would be a very bad thing. Amanda wanted to know what it would be like to feel Nai's tongue on her pussy. To feel Cade's dick rut in her. She suspected a man as large as him could give it to her hard and rough, something she craved but never got from her other lovers. While the oracle, sweet Nai, would be all soft and pliant. A perfect combination.

Cade continued to squeeze her breast while Nai pillaged her mouth. The woman's tongue mimicked the motion of a dick as she feasted on her mouth.

"Shit." Cade snarled grinding his erection into her ass.

A hand brushed her belly, diving under the band of her shorts. Cool, small hands found her throbbing clit and her soaked pussy.

This had to stop. It had gone too far. It was too much for her to take in, to process. Cade and Nai were bonded. Where did she fit in? Did she even want to put her toes into this situation for a good fucking or two? Amanda needed to think, and that wouldn't happen with Cade's dick pressing against her ass and Nai's fingers stroking her pussy.

Pulling her head back ever so slightly, she broke the kiss.

"Wait. Stop," Amanda panted out. "We can't. I can't."

Cade immediately stepped back, and a soft cry left her lips at the loss of his warmth. Then Nai slipped from her pants. Nai brought her glistening fingers to her lips and lapped the wetness from them.

"Mmm, I was wrong. Your pussy tastes even better," Nai said when she finished cleaning her fingers.

Shit. Fuck. Damn. This is real.

"Thank you for the drinks." Amanda's voice wobbled as she gathered her jacket and all but ran out the front door.

Stupid, so fucking stupid. How had she allowed that to continue for so long? She should have rejected them. She should have said, "No thank you." She should have brushed a kiss over Nai's cheek and walked out the damn door then run the hell home— and not her home on the island.

She tugged on her jacket with more force than she meant to while trudging the short distance between bungalows. The frigid air did nothing to cool the ardor flowing through her veins. It took every ounce of self-control to continue down the walkway and not turn around. What the hell had she been thinking?

You weren't. You wanted what happened. You craved what they gave you. And, if you're honest with yourself, you liked it.

She did. More than liked it. She'd felt so alive sandwiched between both oracle and bear. The supple curves of Nai's body combined with the hard press of Cade's had sent fingers of pleasure through her. Her body hummed with unspent energy.

"Stupid, this is so.... You're so stupid." She trudged on. "Why did you—?"

She bumped into a thick mass of muscle and stumbled. The hard body grabbed her, steadying her. "Whoa, Mandy. Where's the fire?"

Ben. She closed her eyes, and rubbed them. "Sorry."

"It's okay. I just came from your cabin."

"I made plans." The lust strumming through her body agitated her.

"Want to talk about it?"

"Yes." *No.* Why did she want to talk about it? "It's complicated."

"Well, I've got time." He shrugged

"What about Molly? Don't you want to check on her?" The little pre-cog, telekinetic woman had spunk, even if she hid it from everyone. She felt the yearning in the girl to be *better*.

"I did. She's settled in for the night, and I'm going to have breakfast with her in the morning," he replied.

"Oh." She climbed the stairs to her cabin then she turned to him. "What would you do, if you were asked to be the third in a relationship?"

"You mean a ménage?" He stopped inches from her. "Depends I guess."

"On what?" She stepped onto the balcony and walked to her door.

"Whether or not I like them," he answered, following her.

"Okay, so you like them. Then what?"

"Go for it," he stated. "Why would you wait? As long as all three of you know the parameters, it's all good."

"What if the two people asking you to join them are already in a relationship?"

"Same rules apply." He touched her shoulder. Amanda had learned over the years not to flinch. Not to react. "Where did this come from?"

"Cade and Nai," she said.

"You'd be stupid not to go for it," he answered. "That guy has got it bad for you."

"Don't I know it," she muttered.

Ben laughed. "You can do it the easy way or the hard way. Fight and claw against a grain you know you want to follow. Or varnish it."

"Varnish it?" She arched a brow.

"Yeah," he said. "Shine it up. Make it pretty. Stand back and enjoy it after putting the work in."

She shoved into her place. "Fuck."

"It's not so bad." He patted her shoulder and strolled inside.

"So you say." She shut the door behind him. "I'm not quite as optimistic."

"Instead of overthinking it, and looking at the down side, why don't you embrace it? Call it a once-in-a-lifetime opportunity, and if it doesn't work, you experienced something you probably wouldn't out in the field."

It made sense. "Why are you being rational?"

"Because I have this week to figure my shit out or quit. It's given me some perspective."

"How is your knee?"

"Still got a hitch in it, but feels strong." He shrugged, but it didn't cover the thread of worry she felt rolling off of him. There was more; however, she wouldn't push it.

"Good."

"I guess so." He settled on the couch

She threw herself down beside him. "Boy, aren't we a pair."

He chuckled. "Yeah we are, but I wouldn't have it any other way."

Chapter Seven

"That went really fucking well." Cade growled out in pure frustration while Nai sat ever-so-patiently watching the closed front door—almost like she expected Amanda to come back.

"It went as it was supposed to." Nai turned to face him. "You're just sexually frustrated is all.

"And you aren't?" he asked as he began to pace around the room looking for control.

"Oh, I am. But unlike you, I have better control of my...needs." Calm oozed from Nai.

"Bullshit. I've known you too long. Your needs match mine."

Nai sighed softly and nodded her head in acknowledgment. "You must go to her. Talk to her and soothe her fears."

"Me?" He stopped, glaring at his bonded. "That might not be a good idea. You get people way better than I do."

"Pfft," she proclaimed as she waved a dainty hand through the air. "You get her. Right now she needs something from you I can't give her."

What the fuck is she talking about? "Explain," he

demanded.

"I cannot."

"Fuck. I'm worried about blowing this with her, and with you."

"You never have to worry about me. I'm here and I'm staying, even if Amanda does not join us." His heart squeezed at the thought of not bringing her into the fold as the third in their bonding, though.

"You must go to her. But you must calm yourself and control your desires. Come." His bonded patted the seat next to her on the couch.

Walking over, he knew what his bonded was about to do to him. She wanted to help alleviate the desire running rampant through his blood and to help calm the growling bear clawing at his insides.

"Nai—"

"Shh. Trust me." In a graceful move, she straddled his lap. The layers of silky material gathered about her waist and thighs flared out, before falling in hypnotic tiers of fabric. A groan escaped him as his groin fit perfectly into the V of her legs. Warm, soft and, most important, wet. Their little warrior had gotten to her, too.

"This isn't a good idea."

"It is a perfect idea. Your beast must be calmed." Nai took his hands and placed them on the small globes of her ass. His fingers automatically clutched the flesh while he ground his cock against her pussy.

"Fuck." He growled when she rolled her hips, caressing his dick through layers of clothes.

"Relax." She leaned forward to gently kiss his lips while delving under his shirt to pat his overheated flesh. Cool little fingers had his muscles clenching in both anticipation and need as she rubbed her thumb across his nipple.

Nai peppered kisses across his brow, lips, and cheeks before nuzzling him in a sensual dance.

He slid his right hand up from her ass to the hem of her skirt, where he bunched up the long length to gain access to her sex. He shuddered. At some point she had removed her panties. *Fuck, give me strength.* Cade ran his fingers along the outside of her folds then brushed her clit with his thumb.

"Kiss me," he demanded.

"As you wish." Her soft lips touched his and Cade fisted her hair, holding her in place as he devoured her in an all-consuming mating of the mouths. His fingers slipped from her clit, to tease her entrance. Warm and wet, the muscles of her pussy clamped down on his intrusion, trying to keep him in place. Nai gasped, breaking the carnal kiss.

"So wet, my *hjarta*." He sank his fingers into her pussy, while using his thumb to tease her clit.

"This is about calming you." He didn't miss Nai's stern tone.

"It'll calm my beast to know he has pleasured his bonded." Her hips rocked over his groin as he increased the pressure on her clit. The pace of his fingers sliding in and out of her passage quickened until she was writhing in his arms.

Cutting off her protest, he shifted her in his arms—lifting her slightly to capture her hard nipple through the thin barrier of her dress.

"Oh fuck." Nai groaned. The muscles of her pussy milked his fingers as her cream coated his digits.

Releasing her nipple, he continued to finger fuck her, increasing his pace. He'd gotten a taste of her release, and he wanted more. "Come, Nai. Come for me. Then I'll suck your juices from my hand, just like you licked yours clean of Amanda's juices."

She screamed his name as her release coated his fingers.

"*Ek ann per*," he cooed to her as she fell forward onto his chest.

Long moments later, she reached up to cup his cheek. "I love you, too," she whispered, her voice still husky from her climax.

Cade removed his fingers from her pulsing sex, brought them to his mouth, and sucked them clean. "Are you sure about this, Nai?"

"Yes, I am sure." She sat up so they were looking at each other. Her gaze held no hint of doubt or worry. Only excitement and anticipation. "You must trust me."

"I do."

"Enough time has passed. You must go to her now," she proclaimed, rising from his lap. "Are you calm now?"

"Calmer." His dick, which had been aching before, now throbbed with need.

"Then go to her."

"I want you there. I won't bond her without you."

"Silly bear, I will come when the time is right," she stated as she fixed her dress. "As you know my needs equal your own."

***

Cade paced outside for a good fifteen minutes. The soft glow emanating from Amanda's cabin had silhouettes dancing on the paper screen partitions. Their rooms matched almost to a tee.

He also smelled the human, Ben, since he'd been there as well. Cade's bear snarled in outrage, and, if allowed, he'd have pissed a territorial circle around what he considered his.

As he climbed the stairs, he tried desperately to figure out what he'd say to Amanda. Sorry didn't seem good enough. *I want to keep you* sounded stalker-ish. They needed a level playing field. When he got to her door, he knocked and waited. They had to take this slow.

"What did you forget th—"

"I thought we could talk," Cade said.

She paled. "About?" Her grip tightened on the wood, her knuckles turning white from the strain.

"Earlier. I needed to apologize."

"For what?" Damn. She wasn't going to make this easy on him.

"I think we went a little fast. I think we all want the same end result, but we don't know how to get to them," he replied. "I'm sorry if we made you uncomfortable."

"You didn't." She stepped aside, allowing him entry. "It takes more than my fingers getting sucked to make me blush."

Sure it did. The way her chest and cheeks had pinked and her breath hitched.... Yeah, he knew better. "Well if it's all the same," he hedged, "I'd like to say I am sorry. Nai...well, when she sees what she wants, she takes it. Consequences be damned. I have to believe it's due to when and where she was born."

Amanda shrugged. "Nothing bad about knowing what you want."

"Do you know what you want?" he added quickly.

"Some days, yes. I do. Others, not so much. Today is a not-so-much day."

"Want to talk about it?" He had an in with her, and now he needed to keep his feet firmly planted in her personal space.

"I thought you were only here to apologize." She gave him a wary look while curling up on the couch.

"I did and I have. But you appear to need to talk. I'm a good listener." *Better lover.* He reached for her foot, only to have her flinch away from him. "I won't bite. Yet."

That did it. She smiled. His heart lodged in his throat, and his groin tightened. "Nai likes her feet rubbed. She says it soothes her mind and relaxes her body. I do it because I can't keep my hands off of her."

"Are you saying you also can't keep your hands off of me?"

Cade shrugged. When he reached for her foot a second time, she relented, allowing him to extend her leg. "This is new for me. I hated the touch of anyone when Nai and I were first married. It chafed my bear. It's like an irritating sound. You know it's coming from somewhere around you, but you don't know exactly where or how to shut it off."

"And now?"

"I ache to touch you," he replied.

"This shouldn't be happening, Cade. You're a bonded bear. Your responsibility to Nai trumps my need to get laid."

"We fuck," he said. "Getting laid is a meaningless fuck. When we make love, it'll mean more than you can imagine. Our souls will touch."

"Para Elite training tells us about bonding," she said. "You and I can't bond."

"Why's that?" He dug into her arches, loosening the taut muscles.

"You're already bonded."

"True, but there are exceptions to the rule," he

said.

"What kind of exception?"

His bear settled him, relaxing marginally while he continued to talk to her. His fingers caressed and worked her feet until she eased into the cushions of the couch, and didn't watch him like a suspicious cat might.

"For instance, when a mate is too young. Or they are too far away. Or when you don't know about the person until you see them. Or a vision."

"A vision?" She laughed a bit.

"Oracles have visions," he reminded her.

"So are you saying Nai saw me in a prophecy?"

He considered her for a second then nodded. "Something along those lines."

"Interesting."

"It is. The day I met you, I couldn't stop thinking about you. Couldn't stop picturing you naked or wondering what you'd taste like."

"I think we're getting off track." She let out a shuddering breath.

"We're right on track." He lifted her foot and pressed his lips to the side before leaning in and placing kisses across her supple flesh.

"Cade." She whimpered.

The sound shot straight to his cock. His balls grew heavy. Hell yes, he craved this. "I've got you, Amanda."

"That's what I'm worried about," she groused.

He chuckled. "I imagined what your thighs will look like holding my head in place as I eat your succulent pussy."

"Oh God." She closed her eyes.

Cade inhaled deeply, the sweet mouthwatering smell of her pussy calling to him. He pressed his thumb into her arch as his other hand rubbed slowly up her calf and then the back of the knee. He smiled when she gave a little whimper.

"I've also imagined on more than one occasion how your pussy will feel wrapped around my dick. Shit, Amanda I bet you'll milk the cum right out of my balls." He growled as he pulled her closer. "Or how fucking hot it will be to watch you eat Nai out while I'm fucking you from behind."

Her hand jerked up and pressed hard to his chest. "Cade. God, please."

"Are you begging me to stop, Amanda?" His fingers brushed her jeans-covered sex. He swore he could feel the heat from her pussy through her clothes.

"Don't stop." Her thighs tightened around his searching hands and he chuffed, his bear content with the fact she'd begged him.

"Let me have you. I'll give you what you want and need." Nudging her thighs apart, he leaned down to nuzzle her covered sex. "You smell so damn sweet. I could lose myself in this pussy. Eat you for hours and never get my fill."

"I want—" Amanda gasped and Cade couldn't help but smile in satisfaction. She would be theirs.

"I know what you want. I know exactly what a woman like you needs. You want me to fuck you. Hard and fast till you can't think about anything but pleasure."

"Cade!"

"Say yes and it's all yours. Everything you need and desire." Deep growls flowed up from his chest. It was a sound that had only, until now, occurred only with Nai. For him though, it confirmed everything Nai had stated. Shifting Amanda even farther down on the couch, Cade pushed her shirt up and over her breasts and licked a pebbled nipple through her bra.

"Yes," she panted out.

Not wasting another second, he jumped off the couch and scooped her up. He loved the feel of her in his arms, heavier and different from Nai, but just as fucking good.

"Not on the couch. The first time won't be on the couch," he proclaimed as he walked down the hall to her bedroom. He made sure to leave the door open in hopes Nai would eventually join them.

Chapter Eight

Everything happened too fast or too slowly. Amanda didn't know which. One minute they were sitting on the couch, talking, and the next she wanted to touch him. To feel him inside her. Hear his shouts of passion. She craved the ability to connect so fully to another's soul. "Cade," she murmured, when he drew her legs around his waist and leaned in for a kiss.

"Yes," he muttered, before nuzzling her neck.

"What about Nai?" Instead of pushing him away, and denying his touch, she latched onto him and directed him to where she needed him most.

"If she joins us tonight, it will be a celebration." He kissed a path up her neck and across her jaw. "Do you want her to join us?"

Did she? "I-I don't know. I-I mean, she is yours and—" He silenced her with a searing kiss. His tongue thrust into her mouth to tangle with hers, while his hips flexed, pushing his steely erection against her soaked pussy. The hard seam of her jeans rubbed her clit, adding to her excitement.

"She will join us when she is ready. Right now,

this is for us. A handshake of sorts."

"You Canadians have a weird way of shaking hands." She laughed and wiggled over him as he found a particularly ticklish spot on her sides. "Stop. Stop." She giggled. "I'll pee my pants."

"More like cream them." He growled. "I can smell your sweet little pussy getting wet."

"You're so…abrupt."

"Explain," he replied, pulling her shirt over her head then unclasping her bra. "Fucking perfect." He nuzzled her breasts, while cupping the heavy mounds in his hands. His tongue darted out to lap at the sensitive flesh, driving her insane.

"You don't have a filter. You say what's on your mind without fear of repercussions."

"And you don't?" he asked, before drawing her taut bead into his mouth to suck on it. He released the hard point then kissed the valley between her breasts. "I've heard you talk more shit than a Royal Navy Guardsmen on a three-day pass."

"You got me." Her breath hitched and she speared her fingers through his hair, holding him in place. He nipped at the hard peak then drew it into his mouth and sucked.

Amanda saw stars.

"So I do," he teased. "To answer your question, I see what I want, I take it. I want your pussy, so I'm going to take it and fuck it. Make sure you know it's me buried deep inside you." He rolled his hips and groaned. "I'll make you crave it. Beg for it."

Her heart pounded. Her mouth watered. Amanda's eyes rolled back as he explicitly told her what he wanted from her. The more salacious his words, the more turned on she became. "Cade," she whimpered.

His rough chuckle sent a shiver down her spine and settled low in her belly. Her clit throbbed. Her aching sex clenched. If he didn't help her out soon, she'd combust. "What do you want, little human?"

He ran his tongue up her neck and she cried out at the sensation. Holy fuck, she'd never thought she'd like that. She'd seen it in porn and certain movies and got grossed out by it, but with Cade, he lit a fire deep in her belly, arousing her to the point of pain.

"F-Fuck me. Hard. Fast. Make me come. Anything." She closed her eyes as she arched to him.

"As you wish," he whispered before working open her pants. He removed them with ease. She peered down at his hands, at the first prick of pain. Giant bear claws shredded the silk of her panties, ruining her best pair while leaving the slightest scratch. She didn't care though.

He lay down on the bed and fit her thighs around his face. "You smell even better now." The first lick sent a jolt of electricity surging through her body. By the second, she was coming hard. Amanda bucked, riding the waves of her release while Cade's slurping took her higher. "Fuck yeah," he snarled. "Love how responsive you are. Love your taste. I could get drunk on your cream." He fit two of his broad fingers into her entrance and pushed forward." Do it again, Amanda. Come on my hand then I'll fuck you. Hard. All night."

Amanda did something she had never done with any other lover before but knew somewhere deep in her soul that she could with him. She let go, let her body take over and shut her mind down so that she could experience true pleasure. Her pussy rippled around Cade's intrusion when she felt them being pulled from her.

"No...don't stop." Amanda laid a hand on his head.

He chuckled. "I'm not stopping. But in order to finger fuck you, I do need to pull them out a little."

"Oh...my." She panted as her hips jerked and he pushed back into her then pulled them back out, over and over again until her body exploded around him.

"Fuck you're tight." Cade growled as he nudged her legs apart even more and settled between them. The flick of his tongue against her clit had her entire body jerking as pleasure zinged through her womb. "Damn, you're wet."

"More, Cade. I want you inside of me. Please." She cried out as he rubbed at the spot located right behind her clit.

"Not yet. You need to be soaked." He latched onto her swollen clit and sucked it while he rubbed at the sensitive bundle of nerves.

"Yes, now," she demanded as he continued to push her higher and higher. "I need to feel your cock in me!"

"You need to be ready."

"Uh, news flash. I'm not a virgin." She attempted to pull his massive body up and over her. It didn't help that he didn't budge.

"I'm aware of that. But I also doubt you've ever had a man as big as me." Smugness filled his words.

Amanda to pushed up on her elbow and glared at him. "Cocky much?"

"If that means do I have a big cock, then the answer is yes, I do. Now be silent and let me enjoy your sweet little pussy." Cade growled as he went back to gently licking her pussy.

Why did she want to rush this? Oh yeah, because he promised her something she'd never experienced before—a hard fuck.

"Watch me eat you," he snarled. The vibrations ricocheted through her body.

"That snarl is entirely too dangerous." Amanda panted as her gaze zeroed in on his ice-blue eyes. A long, pink tongue ran up and down her slit as Cade feasted on her flesh.

"Your pussy is just as dangerous. I can't wait to feel you wrapped around my dick and milk the cum right from my balls."

Hell, this man excelled at dirty talk.

Cade slowly pulled his fingers free then cleaned the glistening digits. He then kissed his way slowly up her body. Sitting back, he removed his shirt then stood and shucked his jeans. She gaped at him. Boxer briefs encased his large, thick erection. *Holy fuckballs.*

Hooking the edge of his briefs, he pulled them off. His erection lay against his belly. She didn't know where to look first. His long, straight shaft or the sac beneath it. Had she gotten in over her head? His hand wrapped around the twitchy length and stroked. Oh. Fuck. Yes. Her nostrils flared as he jerked himself off in front of her. Anticipation slithered through her.

Fucking finally.

Cade loomed over her, settling between her legs. He pressed his large erection along her pussy, prodding her entrance in a steady rhythm. Yeah, he hadn't been was about his size.

"Now what are you doing!"

"Getting my dick wet," he grunted.

"I think I'm wet enough for both of us." Amanda lifted her legs to wrap around his trim hips.

Cade chuckled. "Are you always this impatient?"

"Patience is not really part of my vocabulary." Rocking her hips ever so slightly, she gasped when the head of his dick settled into her pussy.

"Well, I require it. When I sink my dick balls deep inside you, I'm doing it in one thrust and I'm not waiting for you to adjust to me before I follow through on my promise." He shifted again. "Therefore, we both need to be well lubricated. Unless"—he glanced up from where they were almost joined to catch her eye—"you enjoy a certain amount of pain with your pleasure."

"I'm neither for it or against, as it's not something I've ever experienced," she admitted.

"You mean pain or pleasure in general." Cade paused.

"I mean both."

His blue eyes widened at her admission.

"Most men aren't really waiting in line to date a woman who's six feet tall, has auburn hair, and knows at least a dozen or more ways to kill them."

"Then their loss is totally my pleasure." He placed her right leg then her left, over his arms so that they rested at his elbows. It made her feel completely open and exposed.

Pressure gathered at the opening of her pussy as he shifted and began to push into her ever-so-slowly.

Amanda gasped when more of Cade's cock sank into her. They had just started and already he stretched her to the max.

Leaning over her, he rested his massive hands on the bed and, with a loud growl, powered into her. "Fuck! Damn! Shit!" he shouted as the muscles in her pussy spasmed around him. "You fit me like the tightest fucking glove." And, true to his word, Cade allowed her very little time for her body to assimilate to his, before he began to move in a rhythm as old as time.

He powered in and out, of Amanda, and she finally experienced passion she'd only dreamt about. He grunted above her as his hips slammed against hers. When they were done, she would be sore and stiff, but she would welcome it, because it meant she had been well loved. Even though she hadn't known him very long, she did feel love oozing from the big polar bear shifter.

"Come on my dick. Coat it with those sweet juices." Cade panted as sweat ran down his face and dripped onto her chest.

"Cade!" Amanda cried while another orgasm rushed through her body. "More. Harder!"

"As you wish." He increased his pace.

The air between them was heavy with the scent of their fucking. The wet sucking sounds of his dick pounding into her should have embarrassed her, yet she found it highly erotic.

"That's it. Give it to me. It's mine. Only mine."

With each thrust, the base of his cock rubbed her swollen, sensitive clit. Her body...her mind was in sensory overload and she loved it! She cried out, as her entire body jerked and shuddered.

Cade leaned down, captured one of her nipples, and scored it with his teeth. Her release shot through her, stealing her ability to breathe or even form a thought. Cade moaned in approval.

A cry escaped her when he abruptly removed his dick and flipped her over onto her belly. Massive hands wrapped around her hips and pulled her up onto her hands and knees. In one stroke, he filled her again.

"Fuck, yeah," he grunted.

Glancing over her shoulder, Amanda watched as his gaze locked onto where they were joined.

"That's a beautiful sight for sure." He spread her cheeks apart, staring at her in the most intimate of ways. "Just like I'll never get tired of eating this pretty cunt, I'll never get tired of fucking it." He pressed his thumb to the rosebud of her ass.

"Cade…."

"Shh, you are mine. It is my duty to pleasure you in all things," he reassured her as he sank the thick digit past the tight ring of muscles.

"Correction, she is ours." Nai's soft, husky voice broke through Amanda's sexual haze. A glance at the bedroom door showed a naked oracle resting beside the jamb. Cade kept fucking Amanda.

Nai's lithe little body was utter perfection. Amanda licked her lips in anticipation of tasting the treasures of Nai's body. Especially her pussy.

"She's waiting for an invitation," Cade informed her, slowing his thrusts to a leisurely pace as he continued to work his thumb in and out of her puckered hole.

"I've never…I don't know how to pleasure a woman," Amanda admitted.

"It's as easy as pleasuring yourself," Nai announced from her position by the door. "You experiment, learn what your partner likes and enjoys. You could also do to me what you enjoy yourself. It's no different than loving a man, except I don't have a dick."

Cade chuckled behind her.

Too much. She couldn't think. The way Nai glided toward her, along with the shuttling of Cade's cock in and out of her pussy, put her on edge. "So…so lick you? Bang you with my fingers? Isn't…don't you...don't you feel gypped?"

Nai laughed as she slid up onto the bed and pressed a kiss to Cade's wide back. "I never feel 'gypped,' as you say," Nai said. "Do I, Cade?"

"Never." His cock throbbed inside Amanda while he continued to make soft, pained sounds.

"Are you curious?" she asked, as though she read Amanda's mind.

"Yes."

"I'm rubbing his prostate," Nai said, matter-of-factly. "He loses it when you play with it. Don't you?"

"Fuck," he spat. "You're supposed to be getting your pussy licked, not getting me off."

Amanda laughed.

"Don't fucking laugh." He yelped. "Feels too good. Way too fucking good."

She felt the drag of his cock along her sensitive muscles, whipping her arousal into a brutal storm of sensations that crashed through her. *Oh God. This is really happening.* Her dark-berry colored of nipples captured Amanda's attention. The desire to lick the oracle's tips and, watch them turn hard so she could pinch them, flowed through her. Behind her, Cade cursed.

"What did you do to her, Nai?"

The oracle laughed. "Nothing. She is staring at my nipples." She ran her fingertips over the hard beads then gave them a good tug. "I think she wants them."

"Fuck yeah she does. She went slick around me. Taste her, little human."

Nai shifted closer before guiding Amanda to her breast. "Lick me, firebrand."

Bracing herself with one arm, Amanda wrapped the other around Nai. She mouthed the soft curve of her breast then ran her tongue over her nipple. The point pearled under her ministrations. Curious, she blew on the point and watched it tighten further.

The oracle's soft gasp spurred Amanda on. Again she ran her tongue around Nai's areola then added a puff of air. Nai fisted her hair, guiding her over to the neglected nipple. The flesh puckered, straining upward. Amanda watched in fascination before beginning to tease her again.

Cade growled. His pace quickened while he muttered curses. "Lay her out. Taste her pussy, little human."

She followed the oracle down, changing the angle of penetration and cried out, shuddering as sparks of pleasure shot through her. In this position, he was huge, filling her to the point of exquisite pain. His fingertips dug into her flesh. Tomorrow, she'd wear his marks.

"You smell like irises and jasmine." Amanda placed a kissed to the oracle's thigh. "Lotus," she whispered before drawing the tip of her tongue through Nai's folds. "Anise." Surprise lit her. She'd worried she wouldn't enjoy it. But, with Nai...well, she'd stay between her thighs forever.

She held open the oracle's pussy and lapped at the sweetness coating the hard nub of her clit. She drew the bud into her mouth and sucked on the slick flesh. Nai directed her while Cade's thrusts increased in power.

Amanda cried out. Her body hummed with arousal. Her pussy clenched as she licked and sucked at Nai's swollen sex. Like Cade, she added her fingers, curling them as she retreated. More of the oracle's sweet wetness coated her fingers along with her lips as she fell into rhythm with him. They worked in tandem, building the unbelievable bliss growing between them. Pure energy crackled in the air, and she fed off it. The purity of it. The whiteness of the heat. It surrounded Amanda, sucking her under while she continued to feast on the woman below her. Then, she felt it. Love. Through the layers of pleasure, euphoria, and passion, their love shone. It wrapped around her and yanked the breath out of her. She cried out, bucking against Cade.

His rough, "Fuck," spurred her on. She doubled her effort until Nai clamped down on her fingers. The rhythmic pull, milking her. The awe of it then the sweet reward of knowing she made Nai feel this way.... She turned the woman on and gave her pleasure.

"Please," she cried out. "I need."

"I know you do, little human." He pressed a kiss between her shoulders. "We come together."

"Yes," she sobbed.

Working Nai faster, Amanda's climax built. The energy of the room snapped across her skin. The world spun around her, until she screamed. Her release rushed through her. Brilliant white light flashed before her at the same time as she curled her finger once more and nipped the hard bundle of nerves.

Nai jerked and cried out. Nai's body trembled while Cade filled Amanda once more and roared. They fell into a heap, trying to catch their breath. Cade clutched her. The throb of his release still filling her. Nothing had ever felt so good or made her feel so alive. "Wow," she whispered.

"Wow indeed, firebrand." Nai grinned.

Chapter Nine

Amanda sipped a cup of steaming coffee while she waited for everyone else to arrive on the training field. Getting out of bed this morning had been rough, and she had delayed as long as possible. It hadn't helped that Cade lay pressed to her back, the first time she woke, while Nai had been spooned against her front. She had fallen back asleep, only to wake to find Cade long gone but Nai still cuddling her.

She couldn't the help the smile that floated across her lips as she recalled the good morning kiss she had shared with Nai. It had been intense and left her poor sore sex aching with need. One that couldn't be fulfilled because she only had enough time to get a shower, brush her teeth, and dress before heading out to the field. She didn't worry, though, because Nai had promised a repeat performance tonight.

"Well, look who the cat dragged in." Amanda turned as Cade's deep timbre broke through the quiet on the field.

"I'll have you know I was awake before you or Nai. I just chose to go back to sleep." Amanda took another long sip of her coffee while he moved to stand in front of her.

"Uh-huh."

"It's true. I was an Amanda sandwich this morning." Hell, it never had been this easy to speak to her lovers the following morning.

"If we hadn't had to be here this morning, I would have had breakfast in bed. I craved more of your sweet pussy." He leaned down to rub his nose on and around hers.

Amanda groaned at the slight touch. "Cade! Rekkus can hear you, you know!"

"Then he'll think I'm the luckiest fucker in the world." Warm, hard lips touched hers in a kiss as carnal as the one she'd received from Nai earlier. Her clit pulsed, and her pussy began to moisten. Cade released her lips, gasping. "Fuck, the smell of your pussy is intoxicating."

"Later," she promised.

"You sore?"

"Uh." Amanda could not prevent the flush warming her face at his questions.

"It's a simple question. I fucked you hard," he said matter-of-factly. "All night. So I want to know if you're sore."

"Can this be one of the times you're not so blunt?" Embarrassed, she refused to look him in the eye.

"Can't change who and what I am. Best get used to it and stop trying to change the subject. Answer my question."

"Geez, you're a pain in the ass!"

"Not yet, but maybe one day?" he teased.

"Uh, yeah. Before this conversation goes off the rails, like it is at the moment, yes, I'm sore. But not enough I won't be waiting for you tonight or after lunch or after training. If you want."

Finally, Amanda lifted her head. Her breath hitched. Desire, need, and something else swirled in the blue depths of his eyes.

"Nai has some cream she occasionally uses. I'm sure she could rub it into your tender parts. I'm told it works wonders."

"If Nai were to rub anything into my lady bits, I'm sure we'd end up making love."

"Of that I have no doubt." He smirked. "You done with your coffee?"

"Yup."

"While we wait for the others to get their lazy asses here, want to warm up?" Cade reached out and took the paper cup from her hand. After crumpling it, he chucked it over to the trash can.

"Works for me. It'll help ease some of the stiffness."

"I know something else that's stiff. You're more than welcome to work that out, too."

Laughter bubbled up inside of her. "I'm going to ignore your comment," Amanda quipped.

"You won't be able to ignore me later."

"I don't plan on ignoring you...later!" Amanda settled on a mat to stretch. "Can I ask you a question?"

"You can ask me anything, little human." He plopped down next to her then held his hand out to her. The single touch from his hand had a bolt of need shooting through her body.

"I don't think I've heard you talk so much before. What's changed?" Spreading her legs out in front of her, Amanda gingerly leaned forward to grab her toes. The muscles in her inner thighs protested.

"I'm not usually very vocal, except with those I trust." He watched her intently.

So you trust me?"

"Yes." He mimicked her position on the mat.

"I feel honored." She smiled.

"You should. Trust is hard for polar bears to come by. We don't particularly like humans. We usually only trust those in our immediate family and our bonded."

"You have Nai."

"Yes, I have Nai." He stood, facing away from her.

"She's your only family?"

"And our son."

"I'm sorry. I shouldn't have asked. It's none of my business." Standing, Amanda moved to his side.

"You have every right to ask me. Especially after last night." He took a seat on a bench at the edge of the field then patted the weathered wood. "Join me and I'll tell you my story." She sat next to him and immediately felt a blast of his body heat. "My mother, father, and several older brothers were taken from me many decades ago."

"Oh, Cade." She placed a hand on his thick forearm in comfort. "What happened?"

"Yellowknife is beyond freezing during the winter. Most of the time, my family would have hibernated like real bears to keep from having to hunt in the frigid conditions. I still don't know why they didn't the year after I mated Nai, or if my bonded knew, but I got a call from a member of our sleuth while in Chile celebrating our one-year anniversary. My parents and brothers went out hunting, and a couple of hunters mistook them for real bears. Because the bullets were lodged in their bodies, they couldn't heal. Their frozen bodies were found right where the hunters said they shot them when Fish and Wildlife arrived." He looked away. "The hunters were charged with hunting without a permit. The bodies of my family were released to me, when I requested to bury them. No one even questioned me. I guess they figured I was some weird nature person."

Nausea welled up in her stomach as he described the horror of what happened to his family. It'd been a long time since she allowed others in. Wave after wave assaulted her. Fighting through the cloud of anguish, she focused on his words; otherwise, it would overwhelm her.

"How old were you?" she asked, laying her hand on his. Through the simple touch, she could also help him heal.

"Twenty-five." Cade took a deep breath. "I fell into a deep depression. I lost everything and, goddess love my Nai, she tried so hard to comfort me in my time of need. I pushed her away. Of course, it was ridiculous to think I'd be capable to keep her at arm's length." He grinned. "We had our son two years after my parents' and brothers' death. He brought me out of my stupor." Cade gave her a small smile. "When Nai sets her mind to something she is a force to be reckoned with."

Amanda slowly let out the breath she had been holding as his pain lessened and transformed into love. Love for his bonded and love for his son.

"And, at some point, you joined the Canadian Army?"

He nodded. "Yes. I did," he said. "I was seventeen when the war started. The same year Nai showed up in Yellowknife. My parents adored her and promised to take care of her while I was gone. If you listen to her, though, she cared for my parents, giving them updates when she had her visions."

"Wow."

"Yeah, wow. She showed up in the middle of fall, wearing the same getup you see her in today."

"But, that far north, it's cold and snows and there's ice. How did she not freeze?" Though an oracle, her status didn't make her impervious to the elements. The freezing cold should have killed her.

"She found us in time." He shrugged. "She said she knew where she was heading and knew we'd find her."

"She's pretty confident."

"She is an oracle," he replied.

"Where is your son now?" she asked.

"Here for training. You've met him."

"I have?" She scrunched up her nose, confused by his statement.

"Spike is our son."

Whoa. "Did he get hurt?"

Cade shook his head. "The object of his lusty affection works for the island. Since we were coming, he decided to follow along."

"Who's he got the hots for?"

"A woman named Cammie. She was an operator for The Syndicate. But she retired a few years back and came here to work in the herb garden with Sage."

"Wow. You're full of surprises."

"I try."

"Anything else I should know?" she asked, almost afraid of what his answer might be.

"When we're ready, I want you to carry our next child."

Talk about blowing her mind. A kid? She didn't

know if she was mom material; however, the idea of sharing a life with him and Nai didn't really scare her. It felt right. *It's gotta be the sex fucking with my head.* She needed to change the direction of this conversation...pronto. "So, when did you become her bodyguard?

"I always was a bodyguard, of sorts. Always protecting her. Always making sure she had what she needed. Then the Rowans were attacked."

"And you became her Psi-Guard."

He nodded.

"I remember that. I was just going through basic in Para Elite. The attack shocked us all."

"Nai, too. She'd gone so long." He stared off into the distance. "No one knew. Of course, Spike had already joined Para Elite by then. He wanted to guard his mother as well, but they gave him the task of watching out for Cammie, who'd been showing signs of burnout."

"So, you guarded Nai and he became a sentinel for Cammie. Amazing. I thought about leaving my unit to help the Rowan family too, but...."

"Why didn't you?"

She shrugged then crossed her arms. A chill worked through her body. The day so vivid replayed in her mind.

Ben, their unit, and she made their way into the small town. The peacekeeping mission seemed pretty straightforward. Meet with the tribal leader. Offer them money and protection in exchange for information. And the information could be anything. Be it terror related or para related, they wanted the intel.

The town seemed normal. Kids were playing, adults hustling their wares. But it wouldn't last. She could feel it. When a child tossed a ball at her and she caught it, she saw two men talking while the boy continued to play outside. Dressed in all black, they wrapped suicide belts around themselves, muttering prayers, then brought in others. They worked in silence, donning their jackets preparing for an attack.

She sucked in a breath. The boy had left her side, taking his ball with him. The words were right on the tip of her tongue. But to tell everyone would expose her to abilities to Ben, a human and a skeptic. Not that he didn't know about and accept shifters and others, and not like she couldn't trust him. She did. He'd have her back no matter what. But things would change between them and, she had a crush on him but didn't know how to express herself properly. After being conditioned to believe no one would take her assessment seriously, even though empaths and pre-cognition were abilities Para Elite sought, she hid her gift. Buried it deep, so she didn't have to worry about being turned away or cast out from the people she considered family. On this particular day in the desert, knowing full well what might happen, she swallowed the warning and trudged on. She could prevent the maximum amount of damage though. She'd steer everyone away from the white Mosque where they were supposed to meet the village leaders.

She didn't have time. Ben stood closest to the building when the first explosion ripped through the town.

With a shudder, she returned to the present. "Let's just say I'm not a good protector."

"I doubt that," he replied. "I'm guessing whatever happened is why you're here?"

Amanda blew out a breath. "I'm an empath with pre-cog attributes."

"I knew it." Cade grinned. "You felt everything on another level last night besides experiencing the physical part."

"I did," she agreed.

"So what happened to bring you here?"

"Oh look, here comes everyone." She got to her feet. "Looks like we have more people today." She spotted the petite girl with the crazy hair from her painting session the day before and the bigger guy who'd watched her like a hawk.

"A Kodiak and a black bear," Cade huffed. "Interesting, and bonded, too."

"Huh," she murmured. "They make quite a pair."

"Yes they do," he said, stepping behind her. "Morning, Cyrus." He placed his hands on her shoulders and a rush of reassurance ran through her, along with a snippet of what he promised would happen later. "You're late."

Cyrus regarded them as he stopped in front of them then snorted. "And you're a little too sure of yourself, Arcades. Amanda."

"Cyrus," she said with a nod.

"Shall we get started?"

***

Cade trudged back to the cabin on his own, pissed off because Amanda had something else to do. She'd made up an excuse, of course. More had happened than she was telling him. He could feel it in his bones. Add in Ben's knee, and he could put two and two together. He could ask the guy; however, he'd rather hear it from her.

He took the stairs two at a time, needing to discuss with Nai what had happened.

She met him at the door, her features blank and her body relaxed. She only acted this way when she had a vision.

"What have you seen?"

"You're going to push her too hard," she answered, stepping back into their room.

Shit. "Well, what else do you suggest I do? I offered her an opening," he said, stepping into their place. "I even told her about Spike. Speaking of which, have you heard anything out of him?"

"And she took your offer as far as she is ready to." Nai cupped his face in her hands. "She is scared. Afraid of what will happen when she fully accepts herself." Pressing her lips to his, she lingered there for a moment. "As for our stubborn son, he is still watching Cammie from a distance. But he is having fun with these silly games Para Elite is using as team-building exercises."

At least their son was safe, and happy. "So what do we do?"

"Give her more time. We still have four days to convince her she belongs with us."

"The need to bond though," he whispered, rubbing his cheek across her palm before kissing it.

"I know. Soon, my giant beast. We will bring her into the fold soon. Once she knows her worth." She urged him toward her and kissed his lips. "It will work. I see her constantly now. With every vision, her life is entwined to ours even more."

The scent of fresh mint, eucalyptus, and lavender permeated the air. Nai had been making something before he arrived. Curious, he stepped around her, not willing to acknowledge what she'd said yet. Until the person stood before them, agreeing to bond or join them, he didn't consider it a done thing. "What are you making?"

"A tea." She followed him over to the small kitchen. "I have been trying to dry the herbs all morning, but they're being difficult."

"Salty air," he said, taking in the piles of herbs.

"I thought as much." She came up beside him. "Have you met Molly?"

"I have. She played paintball with us."

"She is hiding as well. She is...worse than complicated. I see the human Benjamin helping her through this transition." She grabbed a piece of cheesecloth then started adding the semi-dried ingredients to the middle of it. "I thought something to relax her might help."

"When are you delivering it?"

"Now. Since you've arrived, she'll be back in her room." Nai made three more packs then tied them with twine Myron gave her. "Come with me."

"As you wish, my queen."

Chapter Ten

Nai knocked on Amanda's door around noon. The morning exercises were complete, as Cade already lounged in their bed. His naked form had tempted her to stay, but she had plans. When the door opened, Amanda stood on the other side. She wore a heavy cable sweater, jeans, and her boots. Her hair had been swept back in a severe ponytail, and she smelled of lilac and lavender. A tinge of pink colored her cheeks as her eyes widened in surprise.

"May I come in?"

Amanda stepped back from the door and allowed her entry. When she stepped inside, she looked around. Everything appeared sterile, not lived in or enjoyed. Even the basket of fruit on the counter hadn't been disturbed. Nai frowned.

"So, what can I do for you?" Amanda hedged.

"I wanted you to take a walk around the hot spring with me."

"Oh, uh, sure." She grabbed her jacket. "Did you want to go now?"

"Yes," Nai answered with a small smile. "I thought we could discuss the events of the last few days."

"The events of the last few.... Why?" They headed out, and Nai took her hand, guiding her down the stairs and out to the small wharf first.

"Well, your life has been upended. Everything is different now. You've lain with a woman and man." She slid her gaze over to Amanda and teased, "I'd be surprised if you haven't wondered when you'd turn into a pillar of salt."

"You mean like Sodom and Gomorrah? So, the story is true?"

"More like ashes to ashes. Dust to dust. A volcano erupted and killed everyone," Nai replied.

"So the story isn't true?"

"Depends on who you ask." Staring out over the ocean, she knew the time was right to explain how all of this would work between them. But she had one more story to tell.

"Have I told you about Vlad the Impaler?" Amanda shook her head, and she continued. "Vlad got his name from years of brutality. He was a prisoner of the Turks as a child, forced to carry out the ruler's bidding or face the consequences of his disobedience."

"He was whipped, from what history tells us. Severely. All the slave children were," Amanda murmured as they continued on their journey.

"Yes," she answered. "By the time he reached adulthood, he had become a killing machine. Good at putting the fear of God into his enemies while crushing their armies."

"That's when he started impaling people on pikes. To add a flare to his conquests." She squeezed Nai's hand, seemingly relaxing. With each step they took, more of the tension bled away from Amanda.

Those awful shields she had built around her lowered slightly.

"Yes. So, when he returned home, he was changed. Hell bent on protecting his people and his family from the Turks. I met him the year he married his first wife. The one everyone, including Bram Stoker, affectionately calls Mina, or her incarnation." Nai giggled.

"So, that part of the story is true then?"

"Partially," she answered. "Vlad married Mina before the invasion of the Ottomans and Mehmet II. The battle waged for several days and nights."

"Vlad won," Amanda said. "But someone told Mina he died."

"According to the stories, yes," Nai agreed. "So, Vlad raced home, to find his wife dead, outside, at the bottom of the tower he'd built to keep her safe. He swore an oath right then and there, from this life to the next, he'd find her again."

"This is where his immortality and vampirism comes from?"

Nai glanced up at her when they stopped along the edges of the hot spring. "Supposedly. But there is a deeper meaning there." She removed the scarf from her head before working open the pins holding her sari together. "Sometimes, we must wait through several lifetimes before we find our soul mate. Or, for shifters, their bond mate. I waited thousands of years to find mine, and together, Cade and I have waited nearly eighty years to find you."

Slow and steady had to be their course with Amanda. Nai knew it.

"They say the hot springs can be healing. Both for the physical ailments and the mental. Join me?" Nai held out her hand, shivering as the cool breeze floated across her naked body.

"Ahh." Amanda hesitated then licked her lips when her gaze fell on Nai's form.

"Join me. Then ask those questions running through your head at this moment." Without waiting for her to reply, Nai began to unbutton Amanda's sweater. She slipped it from her lover's shoulders, before placing it on the racks discreetly hidden within the rocks. "A little help would be nice. It is not exactly easy to remove clothes from you or Cade," Nai teased.

Amanda's body jerked as if suddenly she realized exactly what Nai was doing. Toeing off her shoes, she bent over to pull off her socks then wiggled out of her jeans. "Will Cade be joining us?"

"No. Not this time." Nai watched Amanda in rapt fascination while she removed her bra and undies. Lust slammed into her belly and her pussy throbbed with need. "Come. Give me your hand, and we will enter the water together."

Amanda's larger hand rested in hers as they slowly walked to the edge and slipped into the warm water.

"I've been told that benches are on the sides. Let's move to them so that we may talk." They located the naturally formed rock and within minutes both of them were relaxing in the water.

Keeping her eyes closed, Nai could sense the restlessness and uneasiness coming in waves off her companion. Following Amanda's lead, Nai kept silent and waited for her to speak.

"If—and listen, this is a big if—I go through with this, how will it work?"

Lifting a single lid, she watched Amanda take in her surroundings. Her sharp, hawkish gaze took in everything, from the top of the falls, to the paths around them, seeking out anything, she suspected might harm Nai or them. Cade took his job just as seriously, and Nai had no doubts the warrior woman beside her would be as vigilant.

"You know you are safe on the island; therefore you may allow your guard down and unwind," she said.

Amanda shrugged. "Don't avoid my question." She moved her arms back and forth through the warm water.

"I'm not. Just stating a fact."

Her firebrand snorted, sliding her gaze toward Nai. "And to answer your question. This will work like any relationship."

Amanda barked out a laugh. "Call me crazy, but none of my friends or people I know are in a-a...."

"It is referred to as a ménage, my firebrand," Nai supplied when her lover seemed to get caught up on the terminology. "You must first be able to say it, if you are going to do it."

"I'm not stupid. I know what it is. Not everyone is as sexually free as you," she snapped. Nai swore she detected a hint of jealously in her lover's tone.

"I have been around for several millennia. Did you honestly expect me to remain chaste and pure?" Nai asked, not really expecting a response. "You perhaps forget, most of the time I have been on this earth, a woman did not always have a choice who her lovers were. Quite often, sex was forced upon women." Even after all these years, old wounds could still be opened.

"I'm sorry." Amanda reached out and laid a comforting hand on her shoulder and she could hear the sorrow in her lover's voice.

"How were you to know? I have not spoken of it

to you."

She massaged the tense muscles in Nai's shoulders. A warrior woman with a caring soul. It was not something Nai had seen often in her lifetimes.

"Does...does Cade know?"

"I do not lie to my bond mate." Nai smiled. "Although, I have been known a time or two not to relay everything in detail to him. But, yes, Cade is fully aware. Just like he knows of every lover I have ever taken. My life has been long and few things before Cade offered me pleasure. Sex was one of them. I feel no shame as to who and what I am. I accept it. Just like I know the evil forced upon me was not my doing. Those men who violated me hold sole responsibility for their actions."

Silence filled the space between them as she allowed her words to sink in.

Amanda finally broke the silence. "Do I even really need to tell you about my life? Don't you just know it?"

"A common misconception with oracles. I see only what I am supposed to see. No more and no less. Often, I must translate my visions, because they come in flashes and aren't always clear to me. Over the years, I have often been wrong because I misread my visions."

"Somehow I doubt it. You seem to have your shit together."

"Appearances can be deceiving. I have often made mistakes that have changed the course of a man's life and the world. Of course, you only know what you are shown through an object or from touching someone or through a person's emotional state. Whereas I've seen both sides of the coin. And who is to say which outcome is better?" She shrugged. "It is the past, and there is nothing that I can do for it, but learn and move on."

"Would you tell me?" Amanda asked.

"Well, let see. There was one time I informed King George III to not worry about the American Colonies. Britain would win the little war."

Her lover blinked.

"How wrong I was on that one. The American Colonies overcame Britain's rule, and now you have your country." Nai paused, fighting back a wave a sadness as another failure floated through her memories. "I also never saw President Lincoln getting shot. If I had—"

"Did you know him?"

"Yes, but I knew his wife better. I was brought in to be her healer. The poor woman suffered through migraines and depression, which only got worse with the passing of her second son." Tension filled the air as memories of a time long ago filtered through her mind. "If I could have, I would have stopped the shooting, if only to save her sanity."

Again silence surrounded them, and she allowed her firebrand to take the lead. Nai sensed the sexual hunger dripping from her partner.

"You know, you never did answer my question." She shifted on the bench.

"We got distracted," she stated. "Our relationship, if you choose to accept it, will be just like any other. What you're really asking is, will I become jealous if you should find yourself alone with Cade and passion overwhelms you and he fucks you. The answer is no. Just like he will not get jealous if we fuck. There will be times, like the first time, when we will all be together."

A confused look washed over Amanda's features.

"What are you having a problem wrapping your mind around?"

Her lover sighed. "Of not getting jealous if I see you and Cade being intimate together."

"I can assure you till I am blue in the face, but you will never know the answer until you take the leap and see it with your own two eyes." Nai reached out to cup her cheek. "You were not aware, but I stood at the door for a long time watching you and Cade before I joined you. It gave me pleasure to see Cade give you something he could never do with me." A blush stole over her lover's cheeks as she let out a shuddering breath. "Cade fears hurting me with his lust, which is not the case with you. He can allow the polar bear lurking under his skin freedom to, for lack of better words, run free. Rut."

"But...."

"There is no but. We will all get what we desire out of our relationship. You get the roughness you crave from Cade, but you will also get the softness from me." She cupped Amanda's breast, her thumb worrying the swollen bud of her nipple.

"Nai...." She whimpered. Her firebrand changed positions, and her breasts surfaced.

Nai took full advantage. Leaning forward, she lapped at the delicate skin between Amanda's breasts." Cade was correct. You taste sweet," she muttered along Amanda's flesh as she worked toward her nipple. "I bet your pussy tastes even better. I have dreamed of devouring your pussy. Of eating you till your cream coats my tongue." Capturing the bud, she sucked the pink tip between her lips.

"Oh fuck!" Amanda cried when Nai's tongue flicked the bud between her teeth.

She released her lover's nipple with a loud pop. "Let me love you." Amanda brushed her fingers over her flesh, leaving a trail of goose flesh in its wake. Tentative, yet inquisitive, Nai encouraged her by nuzzling her nipple. "There is a ledge behind you. If you place yourself on it, I could feast upon you and learn what drove our bond mate mad with lust."

"Please...." Amanda begged. "I need you."

"Shh, firebrand. I know. Stand for me."

Amanda stood then leaned in to lap some of the water off Nai's body. Nai gave Amanda a gentle push back to the ledge.

Chapter Eleven

Nai had been pensive since she returned to the room hours after she'd left. The replete expression on her face almost tripped Cade up, but the minute she passed him and walked outside, he knew either something wrong happened, or things were on the path they were supposed to be on. He followed her out the door then wrapped her in his arms while she stared out over the ocean. "What is bothering you?" he whispered, nuzzling the back of her neck.

She'd retreated into herself a time or two before. This time, however, it worried him. For long moments, she didn't say anything and he wondered, if by chance she ever would.

"Things are still in the air," she answered. The determined edge and sureness she'd displayed the whole time they'd been on the island, seemed to dissipate.

"So, I take it things didn't go well?"

"On the contrary," Nai replied. "They went...swimmingly."

"But?"

She sighed and turned in his arms. "She needs to

reconcile this on her own. I cannot force it and neither can you. We have to be patient. But how, when the one you desire is floundering with her tattered emotions?"

He wished he had an answer for her question. He didn't. "If I had the answer, I'd be a hell of a lot calmer than I am now."

She laughed. "Touché."

By the next morning she seemed right as rain. They made love as the sun crested the horizon then, afterward, she asked to have breakfast in the dining hall.

"I have something to tell you," she hedged, as they followed the path back to the main part of the resort.

"I suspected as much last night," he replied, tucking her into his large frame. "What's troubling you?"

"I told Amanda about Vlad," she began. "About lifetimes searching for mates and true love."

"How did she react?"

"I'm not sure." She rubbed her forehead. "I believe I made headway. She asked about ménage and my past. The fear of taking something that isn't hers. Her fear is real and palpable, but she is so...."

"Innocent?" He'd felt it, too. For all her hard edges, and the walls she put up between herself and the world around her, she had a softness to her. He wondered if Amanda even realized it.

"Yes." Nai nodded. "She has never, I suspect, let anyone in this far. She is giving us the greatest gift, and she has no clue she's doing it."

"Then we are on the right path with her." Cade opened the door to the dining room and ushered her inside. "I have to admit, when you returned last night, you had me worried."

"I'm sorry, my love," she said, cupping his cheek. "It wasn't my intention. I had a lot on my mind."

"It sounds like it." He pressed his lips to her palm. "What else happened while you were with our little human?"

"We had sex," she answered, while sitting down at the table she'd chosen for them. "She is very...strong. Her body is like yours, muscular under her suppleness. And she tastes of passion."

His cock stiffened at the scent of his bond mate's arousal. "Yes, she is." He leaned in. "Did you eat her pussy, Nai?"

A sensual smirk tugged at her lips. "Of course. I enjoyed watching her climax against my tongue repeatedly."

A growl of pleasure built in his chest. "And you're keeping these details to yourself? You could have told me last night, and I would have recreated your encounter with you."

Nai laughed. "The older you get, the hornier you become."

"Not every day you find out you have two bond mates instead of one. For the last couple of days I've had a perpetual hard-on not even sex is easing."

She took his hand in hers and squeezed. "I feel it, too, and so does Amanda. I am not sure what else we can do, other than bind her to us and prove what we've been telling her."

"Will it work if we bond?"

Nai inclined her head. "Yes."

"Then we should bond with her. Afterward, you and Amanda can show me what I missed while you were away." He bent his neck slightly and pressed his lips to her.

"You have no shame!" Laughter bubbled out of the lips he'd just spent long moments kissing.

"I learned from you." Cade nuzzled the flesh between her shoulder and neck.

"We will have to indulge in those needs later. We must eat." Nai attempted to maneuver out of his arms.

"Spoil sport." Cade eased away from Nai.

"I think," Nai's gaze scanned down his body and rested on his raging hard-on, "perhaps you should find something else to think about. I do not wish all these women in this room to get a look at this." She cupped his erection with her tiny hands. "And have them all rioting because they want a piece of you."

"Yeah, well rubbing my dick isn't helping that!" Cade groaned when he felt her delicate fingers caress his length through his pants. "Fuck, Nai!"

"Not yet. But soon." She released him and reached for her tea. "Perhaps a walk to get yourself some coffee would help?"

"Perhaps," he agreed, standing. "And perhaps I should take you back to our room and fuck till you can't walk." With step Cade took, his jeans rubbed the head of his dick. Adding the imagery of his mate between his potential mate's thighs, licking and sucking her to climax, drove him insane. Damn it, any additional stimulation and he'd be coming in his jeans.

"Nai," he admonished, taking his seat. "The fucking walk didn't help."

Her laughter had his dick pulsing even more. Reaching down, Cade adjusted himself. The thought occurred to him to clear the table and get balls deep inside Nai, but the Rowans wouldn't appreciate that, nor would his mates.

A server placed plates in front of them and he thanked the person, and dug in. Past starving, Cade ate with a voraciousness he'd only experienced when his oracle walked into his life. So caught up in his thoughts he hadn't noticed until he was almost done, Nai hadn't touched a bit of her food. Instead, her focus rested on the door.

"Nai?"

"It is okay." She gave him a small grin. "I am just waiting for Amanda, so that we can share our meal."

"Damn."

"It is all right. I knew you were hungry. You will be able to share your second plate with us." When he'd cleared his plate, he requested another. The moment the server placed it front of him, Nai elbowed him.

"She's here," Nai whispered.

Cade glanced up.

"Don't look at her. She must come to us." Nai picked up her fork and moved food around her plate.

Long moments later, she blew out a sigh of relief as Amanda started for them.

"Hey *Mamī, Pitā jī*," Spike said with a squeeze of Nai's shoulder. "I thought I would join you for breakfast." Their son sat down across from them.

Cade held his breath. Would Amanda change her course or continue on? "Son," he said. "How are things?"

He nodded. "Hungry. Horny. Chuffed. Same as always. *Mamī*, are you well?"

"Uh huh." Her gaze remained on her plate.

"Did I interrupt anything?"

"Morning," Amanda mumbled from across the table.

His slowly wilting erection came back full force.

"Is this seat available?" Cade could sense her pensiveness. "I mean, if I'm not disturbing you."

"We held it just for you." Nai gestured to the empty seat across from her.

"Can I get you a cup of coffee or tea, Amanda?" Cade asked as he stood up and pushed his chair back.

"Coffee. Please. Black with no sugar and two drops of cream."

"Be right back. Nai, Spike?" Cade stopped behind his bonded. "Do you require anything?"

"No. I have everything," she stated.

Cade leaned down and rubbed his nose along Nai's.

"I'm good, Pops. Morning, Amanda. Are you ready for our field test today?" Spike asked, as Cade stepped away from the table.

His son meeting the third to their family couldn't have come at a worse time or a better time. It would make explaining the situation easier. Not that a sixty-five-year-old man didn't know what bonding meant. or sex. His boy, like him, had a hardy appetite.

Returning to the table, the polar bear within demanded he give Amanda a morning greeting. Knowing she wouldn't expect it, Cade placed the steaming mug beside her plate then laid his hands on either side of Amanda's face and gently rubbed his nose over hers.

"It is a sign of affection and greeting," Nai explained. "You will get used to it, and actually learn to crave it. Especially since he's more likely to rub his nose across yours than to kiss you."

"Ah...yeah. Okay." She reached for her cup and, sipping the hot beverage, she eyed them. What went on in her pretty little head?

"How is Cammie, *Putara nū?*" Nai asked.

Spike scrubbed his face. "She is...broken."

Amanda frowned. "Do you need help?"

Their son shook his head. "I'm not sure she is ready. She's stuck in her head." He nudged her. "You know how Molly is, right?"

She nodded. "Yes."

"She reminds me so much of the tiny woman. Cammie has a strong back and a will to live, yet the memories. They invade her waking hours and her sleep."

"PTSD," Amanda murmured. "There are others here who suffer as well. I can maybe help soothe her, if you'd like. Let me know."

Spike nodded, giving her a toothy grin. "You've picked a special one, Mom. Welcome to the family, Amanda." He gave her a quick side hug then stood. "I'll see you on the field later."

Cade watched his son exit the dining room then glanced over at Amanda. "Thank you."

Amanda placed her cup on the table and fiddled with her silverware. Cade didn't miss the bright red flush covering her cheeks or the fact that she wouldn't look him in the eye.

"So, Nai told me you two had a wonderful experience at the falls yesterday. She agrees with me, your pussy tastes amazing. Like passion, I believe were Nai's exact words." Amanda's head jerked up, and her gaze swung between his and Nai's. "I'm sorry I missed it. Watching you sample Nai the other day while I fucked you was one of the best experiences of my life. I'd have loved to watch her eat you out. Especially since I know what she can do with that little tongue of hers."

"Oh," Amanda gasped. Her gaze finally stopped flicking between them then settled on him. Nai placed her hand on his thick thigh and patted it softly. "You're not mad?"

"Fuck, no. Why would I be mad?" he asked, picking up his cup.

"Well...." Amanda stopped, glanced at Nai then back to him. "Well, because Nai gave me pleasure."

"And you finger fucked me to release," Nai interjected, spooning up some oatmeal.

"Shit." Amanda leaned forward and rested her head in her hands.

"Please look at me," Cade coaxed her. "I would never be mad, upset, or jealous about my girls enjoying themselves together. It makes me happy you found pleasure in each other's arms."

"But it was not enough. Was it, Amanda? Something was missing?" Nai interjected. "We both felt it."

"To be honest, I'm really not sure what is wrong with me. Previously, sex was, for lack of a better word, unfulfilling, and I avoided it. Now?" She took a deep breath and let it out slowly. "I can't get enough. I crave it. The need is like a knife clawing at my belly. The moment we were done, Nai, even with it being one of the most pleasurable experiences of my life, I wanted more. I needed more."

Nai squeezed his thigh hard.

"Then we shall give you more." Cade pushed her plate closer to her. "You should eat. You will need your strength. Nai and I are going to fuck you, make you come so many times, you won't be able to move for a good long while."

Cade worried Amanda would bolt from the table and never come back, but she picked up her fork and dug into the breakfast he'd placed in front of her. He glanced at Nai, and relief shone brightly in her eyes.

The woman who sat in front of them would finally be Nai and his bonded mate.

Chapter Twelve

Waiting for both Nai and Amanda to finish eating was pure torture for Cade. Then Nai informed them she wanted to walk back to their cabin. His bear didn't take the news really well. As a matter of fact, it seemed downright pissed off at Nai's declaration. His dick didn't seem too happy about it either; it throbbed and pulsed, pre-cum pooling at the tip. He wouldn't be surprised if he came right in his damn jeans with the nice leisurely pace the girls were taking.

He chuffed, and Nai gave him a long, pointed look. Cade just nodded at her. Amanda would be lucky if he didn't fuck her up against the door the second they entered the cabin. No, it wouldn't work because Nai wouldn't get any pleasure. The floor. Yeah, he'd lay Amanda out on the floor, and sink between those muscular thighs, and feast on her sweet pussy. Nai could straddle Amanda's face so she could eat her out. He really needed to stop thinking about it. Reaching down, Cade cupped his junk and shifted it in his jeans. It didn't help.

It wasn't until they were three-fourths of the way

to the cabin that he noticed Nai glancing over her shoulder at him. A sexy little smirked floated across her lips. She did this shit on purpose. Thank God he had the presence of mind to let Myron know they'd be missing training for the rest of the day. The little bit of a woman grinned and told him she'd let Rekkus know and to have fun. *Crazy ass psychic.*

They would though. Both of them knew Amanda loved a good hard fucking, and she was doing everything she could to make sure it happened. Images of him bonding with Nai flashed through his mind. Their bonding had been slow, soft, and sweet. Well aware of how delicate Nai was, he never released himself full force on her. But Amanda. She would be a whole different story.

Deciding to take the wind out of his bonded's sails, he walked up behind Nai. "The jig is up. I know what you're about."

Amanda stopped and glanced between him and Nai. Confusion flashed across her face.

"I want to make sure Amanda gets exactly what she needs from us." Nai continued down the pathway.

"Well, it's not going to be a problem, right about now. I'm so damn hard, I could pound nails!" Cade snarled, uncaring who heard him as they walked along the path.

"Oh?" Nai stopped. "I thought perhaps Amanda and I could make you harder."

"Shit." The little minx. Paybacks were a bitch, and he'd make sure of it. He'd give her a good show of him screwing Amanda in the future then torture her until she was begging for relief.

"What is going on?" Amanda broke into his thoughts.

His gaze moved from Nai's back to her. "She's amping me up. Or I should say she is amping my beast up," Cade stated, urging them on.

"Why?"

"Because she wants to make sure I give it to you hard. Like you need."

"I swear, you two are going to take a minute to get used to," Amanda muttered, coming to a stop.

"Her heart is in the right place," Cade assured her as he placed his hand on the small of her back to nudge her forward. But, Amanda didn't move.

"That's not what I mean."

"The whole no filter thing again?" He smiled when Amanda nodded. "We would never ask you to change who and what you are. It is how we are and who knows, maybe one day you'll join in," Nai said, placing her hand on the small of Amanda's back.

"Don't hold your breath," she mumbled.

"Don't deny it. You love it when I talk dirty to you. I can smell your sweet, tasty cream the moment I started speaking."

"*Cade!*"

"I love when you say my name, but I love it even more when my dick is buried deep inside you or when I'm eating your sweet pussy."

"It's a losing battle, isn't it?" she asked as she shifted from foot to foot and the scent of her desire grew.

"Yup." Being the impatient bear he was, Cade leaned down and slipped one arm under Amanda's knees while the other went to her back and lifted her into his arms.

Amanda threw her head back and laughed. Damn, her laugh. The deep, husky intonations coming from her sounded almost as sexy as when she screamed his name.

"Do you know what's going to happen?" he asked. Her scent calmed the lust running through his body.

"I have an idea. It isn't like I haven't been around paras before. I've helped them."

"Do you have any questions?"

"Not at this moment, but if one pops into my head, I'll raise my hand and ask," she teased.

Now it was Cade's turn to laugh. He stepped through the open door of his cabin and took in what Nai had done in the few minutes since she had gotten there before them.

The lights were off, shades pulled down, and candles flickered all around the room. Nai had also lit some of her incense. The smell didn't overpower the room; instead it added to the ambience.

"Nai?" He kept Amanda in his arms as he strolled down the hallway to the bedroom. Nai had turned the covers down on the bed and lowered the heat.

"I thought perhaps we could have a drink to celebrate this," Nai held a bottle of champagne in her hand.

"You don't have any glasses." Their potential mate wiggled in his arms.

"Oh, firebrand, there are much more delicious ways to enjoy this champagne than with a glass." Nai wrapped her hand around the cork and twisted the bottle. With a loud pop, the gasses escaped, but not a single drop flowed out of the bottle.

He gave Amanda his attention. "But, first, you're a little over dressed for this." He slipped her jacket from her arms then pulled the knit blouse over her head. "Getting better."

Stepping back, he removed his shirt then his pants with a groan. "Fuck." He cupped his shaft and balls and gave a good tug, trying to ease the ache momentarily.

Out of the corner of his eye, he saw Nai remove her clothes as well. Her slight naked form did powerful things to him. But seeing both of his mates drove him insane. "Stop looking at me like I'm a piece of meat," Amanda muttered, crossing her arms.

"Can't help it," he replied, advancing on her. "I need you. The longer we stand here talking or imagining champagne rolling down your soft, supple flesh, the harder my dick's getting. Pretty soon, I won't have the control I need to complete the bonding."

"So we fuck first," she said, rolling her shoulders. "You can do me from behind then we'll bond."

He shook his head. "Nope, doesn't exactly work that way." Wrapping an arm around her waist, he lifted her. "We all have to be touching. We all have to be connected."

Nai crawled up onto the bed and ran her fingertips across Amanda's nipples. "Your hand in mine. Mine in Cade's and Cade's in yours. When we press our bodies together, the kiss you share with him will complete the bonding. Wrapping your soul with his and mine."

His heart tripped a beat. Nervous energy rolled over him. Threading his fingers with Amanda's, he placed a kiss on the back of her hand. "Ready?"

"I-I guess." She licked her lips. Fire and trepidation swirled in her eyes. Yet, the scent of her arousal increased.

"Let's begin." They joined hands. Pressing his body to Amanda's, he groaned. His cock nestled in the curve of her hip. The warmth of her touch seared him. "Remember, don't back off. The kiss will steal your breath and just when you think you can't take it anymore, our souls will wrap around yours." Nai positioned herself at their side, her tiny form pressed to theirs.

Cade leaned in for the kiss. Energy raced through him. Anticipation curled in his gut. Everything inside of him hummed to life. Their mate. Finally, they'd make this a permanent arrangement. Finally, they'd have their family. He brushed his nose over Amanda's once, twice, then....

"Wait!" Amanda released her hold, before putting distance between herself and them. "I can't do this. I have to tell you something. It'll change everything." She paced the bedroom. Her fingers raked through her long auburn hair.

"What is it?" he asked, shocked, and a little more than confused by her outburst. Had this been what Nai warned him about? When he glanced at his mate, her features were closed off.

"I'm not staying," she said. "I can't stay here." Amanda continued her up and back path, eating up the distance of the room. "It's not fair of me to bond with you if I'm going away."

He narrowed his eyes. "What do you mean, going away?"

"Ben," she started. "He's messed up. He won't admit it. He won't tell anyone yet, but I know. He has to retire."

"And this means?" Nai gently prodded.

"I become commander of our Para Elite unit."

Cade reared back as though slapped across the face. "What?"

Amanda stopped pacing and faced them. "This

119

was a working vacation for me. A way to reconcile my abilities so I don't hesitate anymore and can become the leader."

"And you've accomplished your mission?" Nai asked, sitting down beside Cade.

"Kind of?" She shook her head and made an exasperated sound. "I don't know. I still haven't told Ben the accident was my fault. I put him in the position he was in. If I would have stopped him.... If I would have told him about the bombs, he'd be healthy and fine. We wouldn't be here having this conversation."

Nai gasped beside him. His bear roared in outrage. The logical side of his brain told him Amanda didn't mean her statement to come out as it did. The irrational side said, bullshit, she did. She knew what she was doing from the beginning and had played them like fools. "So, you were using us to get off with? Scratch an itch? A-a notch on your para-pole."

Amanda narrowed her eyes. "What? What the hell are you talking about?"

He stood and pinned her to the wall in a flash. "I said, did you like getting your pussy filled by a bear? Are you one of those fucking groupies who always wanted to know what it would be like to fuck a shifter?"

Her lips curled into a cruel snarl. "For your information, you're not my first shifter. I didn't come here to get fucked by a bear or his oracle. I came here to heal. I-I came here with the full intention of making up for my mistakes, but it's pretty fucking obvious, I keep fucking up."

She tried to push him off her, but he wouldn't budge. He scented no lie from her, but a primal part of him raged at being denied his mates. "You're lying," he said. "You're hiding something."

Amanda snorted. "Don't you know, I'm good at hiding everything? It's why I do my job so well." She shoved him again, this time escaping him. She gave a fleeting glance to Nai. "It's been fun. The sex has been awesome. But I told both of you from the beginning that's all this will ever be for us."

Before he could snatch her up and demand she take it all back, she grabbed her clothes and exited the cabin. Nai sat on the bed, silent tears tracking down her cheeks. His poor delicate mate was falling apart in front of him, and there had been nothing he could do to stop it or protect her. His heart lurched. The need to bond still coursed through his veins, demanding he find Amanda and finish what they started. However, he wouldn't have a mate who went insane because he forced the bond.

"She is lying," Nai said softly.

"She sounded pretty convinced she knew what she was saying," he groused.

Nai nodded, folding her hands in her lap. "I know."

"Is this what you saw?" he questioned, coming over to sit with her.

"Some of it." She nuzzled his chest when he placed her on his lap. "She is afraid. Her lack of trust or fears of rejection have destroyed her relationship with Ben. Her taking his job and allowing him to stay with Molly is her penance."

"So, it's better to hurt us than to tell the truth?"

"The thorn in your paw is blinding you," she said, rubbing his chest. "You are upset, as am I, but so is she. Did you not see it in her eyes before she left?"

No, he'd heard the venom in her voice. Felt each

blow she dealt to him while also listening to his bear cry and his heart break. He held Nai tighter. "I saw nothing of the sort."

"Of course you didn't," she said. "The anguish and heartache in her gaze has gutted me, Arcades. She pushed us away to protect us from her. From her...whatever she fears will happen to us if we choose her and her life."

"We don't need to be protected," he growled.

"I know this and you know this," Nai began, "but Amanda doesn't. The last time she tried to safeguard someone she considered family, she failed. What do you think is going through her mind, Cade?"

"Son of a bitch!" He growled, closing his eyes. He tried to calm the beast within, Nai stroking his back easing the tension between his shoulders. She'd been the only one ever to ease his rage. "So what do we do now?"

"We wait. Remember what I told you. She has to come to us of her own free will. Until she is ready, we can't push her, and we won't force this on her."

"And, when she doesn't, then what?"

"She will," Nai said, her voice filled with confidence. "We just have to give her a little bit more time."

Chapter Thirteen

Amanda paced. She'd come back to the spot she'd seen Ben and Molly occupied for lunch. Only, they hadn't shown up today. Since last night, she'd stayed holed up in her room. Utterly pissed off at herself for fucking up everything, and afraid Nai and Cade wouldn't take her back.

"How stupid can you get," she snapped. "You pushed them away." If they'd left after her tongue lashing, she couldn't blame them. She basically told them to shove off and leave her alone.

"You know," Ben started. "They say the beginning stage of psychosis is talking to yourself."

"Ben," she whispered as a wave of relief rushed through her.

"In the flesh. What are you doing out here? Why weren't you at any of our classes?"

She'd skipped therapy and training, opting instead to binge on ice cream. "Self-loathing," she said. "I spent my time being depressed, pissed off, and hating everyone including myself most of all."

Ben sighed. "What did you do?"

"Oh, you know," she said. "What don't I do?" She

walked over to the bench and took a seat.

"It's not like you to be this cryptic."

"It's a new charm I've acquired," she said. "I might have explained what will happen when this week is over seconds before Cade and Nai bonded with me."

"What?"

"Yeah, great timing right?" She took a deep breath and let it out slow. "I told them I would be the new commander when you retire."

"Wait," he said. "I don't think I understand."

"I told them everything." And now, she was going to tell him the same, only she'd never told him the good part before. "We're here because of me."

"No," he said. "A fucking IED explosion is why we are here."

"One I could have protected you from." She licked her lips as she gazed out over the orchard. "I'm an empath, pre-cog. I saw what we were walking into. I was afraid. I didn't know what you would say. I didn't know how to tell you. I touched a ball from a boy, and I saw it all. The suicide bombers. They were in the building. I tried to stop you before you entered the building, but I froze. I caused all this. I did this to you." She gazed up at him as the anguish radiating from him turned to anger then sorrow. The sorrow didn't make sense. "I told them when you're done here you're going home with Molly and I am going out into the field with our team. You've got a woman now. I couldn't protect you then, but I can now."

"I never took you for a dumbass. Who'd have thought it?" Ben just shook his head as he glared at her.

"Ben."

"Nope. You said what you had to say, now I'm

going to say what I have to say, and you're going to sit there and listen."

Her mouth opened and closed a few times.

"I'm still your commander, so that's a fucking order," Ben snapped. "I got hurt because some jackass couldn't just off himself and leave the world with one less dickhead. Nope, instead he decided to go into a building with the sole intent of killing innocent people. It wasn't your fault, and even if you'd told me, those people still needed to be protected."

"But I should have warned you," she protested.

"How long have we worked together?" Anger radiated from him, and she couldn't blame him. She just informed him she caused of all of his pain. He had every right to be mad at her.

"A decade or more."

"Right, and do you think even if you had told me about what you saw it would have stopped me? I had a mission to complete, and I would have done so come hell or high water. Because it is my job."

Unable to look him in the eye any longer, her gaze dropped. Ben wasn't just her commander, she considered him a friend. They had often spent downtime together and built a friendship she truly cherished. And as if a lightning bolt zapped her in the ass, she realized he told the truth. He would still have gone into that building because it did hold innocent people, and Ben would fight with all his might to save those inside saying their morning prayers. Just like she would.

"I should have told you about my abilities." A quick glance up through her lashes and Amanda saw the look on Ben's face. It was one she had seen often enough when he'd been completely disgusted by something.

"Should've, could've, would've. But I already suspected, Amanda. I have for years."

"You never said anything!"

"Well, I'd kind of hoped you'd finally fucking trust me enough to tell me."

"I have trust issues." Regret filled her at her admission.

"I noticed." His tone softened.

"I'm sorry, Ben. If I'd opened my mouth, you wouldn't be walking away from something you love so much."

"I love Molly more, and I would gladly walk away from everything to have a moment in time with her." Love shone in her best friend's gaze.

"But wouldn't you have preferred to be able to make the decision, rather than have it taken away from you?"

Ben signed. "Amanda, I felt some sort of connection with Molly when we rescued her three years ago. I was biding my time. This"—Ben gestured to his bum knee—"isn't the reason I'm resigning my commission. It's because of Molly and the life I want to build with her. And you also have that chance. Don't continue to be a dumbass and walk away from your bonded. We see the fucking dregs of society and the shit they do to the paras. Don't you want to finally experience what's good in life?"

"But, my job." The words tumbled out of her mouth before she could even stop them.

"What about it? There is no rule, no regulation that states you can't be on the Para Elite if you're bonded. Hell, look at Kaleb and Serena. They're just fine."

"How can I go out on missions and place myself

in danger?" The thought of the pain Cade and Nai would feel if something happened to her, tugged at her heart.

"You could be killed leaving the island for cripes sake. Take back control of your life. Stop allowing fear to rule your every choice and decision. They're your bonded. You should want to be with them both and do whatever you need to do to make that shit happen." Ben plopped down on the bench and took her hand. "Promise me."

"Aren't you the one who told me to basically fuck and have fun?"

"Yeah, well, I was hoping you'd finally break through those damn walls guarding your heart," he stated. "Tell me you don't love them, Amanda. Tell me your heart isn't aching as you sit here with me. Tell me it isn't breaking and I'll get you off the island right now. There's a small boat with your name on it. It'll get you back to your tiny, bare apartment."

Snatching her hand out of his, she rubbed the area where her heart rested. It had been a knee-jerk reaction to Ben's questioning.

"It's too late." A single tear slipped from her eye and rolled down her cheek.

"It's never too late. Go to them, explain why you ran. They'll understand." Ben laid his large hand on her shoulder.

"I hurt them." Another tear slipped free.

"I can guarantee you'll hurt them even more if you walk away without explaining." He squeezed her shoulder.

She sniffed. "No, it's better I leave. For everyone." Her heart cracked in three pieces. The thought of never seeing her oracle or her bear again shattered her. She needed them more than she should have.

"Stop being so damn stubborn. It's okay to be scared. You're allowed to wonder if you're making the right decision." He wrapped his arm around her. "But you have to go back to them. You have to explain or else you'll lose everything."

"When did you get to be wise and shit?" She glanced over at him before wiping the wetness from her cheeks.

"When I got here and saw Molly." He shrugged. "Go to them."

"Fine." She sighed. "I'll go to them."

But how did she tell them? Standing, she waited for him to join her then hugged him. "She's worth it then? Falling in love?"

"Yeah, well worth it. I have my soul mate," he said with a smile. "It feels pretty good."

"You're such a softy," she grumbled.

"Get the hell out of here." He laughed.

"Fine, I'm going." She started back for the beach houses. "You're still an asshole!"

"That'll never change," he hollered.

Her steps slowed as she crested the hill. How the hell was she supposed to fix this? She did love them. More than she ever loved anything. Yet, she'd been so mean. The things she said.... God, she hated herself.

As she topped the small ridge, she saw their cabin and stilled. Going in there meant taking everything they were offering her. Shouldn't she want it? They'd been so patient, so caring, and all she did was shit on them.

"You look lost." Cemil. She'd know his voice anywhere.

"Not lost. More, unsure," she said glancing at him. "Do you think someone who is meant for greater, should be allowed to have it, even though they've done shitty stuff?" she asked.

"I think everyone is destined to have second chances. What they do with it is up to them," he said.

"What if they allowed someone to get hurt?"

"Are we talking about you and Ben?"

"Abstract," she said.

"Well, in the abstract, yes."

"But—"

"No buts," he said. "Here's the thing. You have to let yourself make mistakes. Trust people. Lose the trust you found in them. It's all a part of the evolution of life."

"How do I make up for the shitty things I've said, though?"

"Start by saying, 'I'm sorry.' Explain why you're so messed up then have sex. Blow their minds. Bond. Live." He shrugged when she gave him an incredulous look. "I'm being honest."

"No, I hadn't noticed. Should have lied to me." She snorted.

"I think you've dealt with lies enough," he replied. "Go live your truth."

Amanda nodded. "Okay."

With a wave, she started for their room again. What she'd say when she arrived, or how they'd react, scared her. Nevertheless, she trudged on. She had to tell them they did matter. She did love them. She needed them to know how afraid she was. How much she didn't want to screw up, although she already had. She wanted to tell them she trusted them even though she didn't trust herself. She needed to tell them she loved them and she couldn't live another day without them.

"God help me; I've become a blubbering girl.

Dammit, Ben. You did this to me."

Chapter Fourteen

Apprehension made her stomach churned with unease as she took the steps up to Cade and Nai's cabin door two at a time. She could do this. She had to do this. Lifting her hand, she knocked and waited. When no one opened the door, she began to worry perhaps they had already left and she had lost them both. She stepped over to the window and peaked inside. A wave of relief washed over her when she noticed some of their belongings still lying about. *Maybe they went for a walk, or maybe Cade took Nai to the falls and hot springs to help her relax.*

Amanda tried the door to be sure. Unlocked, it gave way, and she was blasted with a wave of arousal combined with love so strong that it almost brought her to her knees. They weren't at the waterfall; they were still here and, trusting her senses, they were in the middle of an intense fucking. Not willing to let her fears and doubts hold her back, she closed the door, locked it then headed down the hallway toward the bedroom.

Nai rested on her back, while Cade plowed his massive dick in and out her pussy. It excited Amanda.

Her sex grew wetter by the second. Her gaze locked on to Cade's dick, slick and creamy with Nai's juices as he fucked her. Not as hard as he wanted or needed to be, but Amanda knew he would never unleash his full passions on their tiny bonded.

Toeing off her shoes while pulling her shirt out of her jeans, she stepped farther into the room. Her gaze floated between Cade's flexing ass and the spot where they were joined. She wanted this, needed this. To open herself completely up to them and join the powerful energy of their absolute love.

"I love you," Amanda whispered under her breath.

Cade stopped. He glanced over his shoulder, while Nai stared at her through the space where he braced his arm. Fierce need showed in both their gazes, and Amanda finally realized that although they loved each other, their love wasn't complete without her.

Nai slowly lifted her hand, and held it out to her.

"I'm so sorry," Amanda cried out as she scurried over to the bed and took Nai's hand.

"Shh. It had to be this way." Nai tugged her gently down beside her. Cade, on the other hand, hadn't moved or really acknowledged her presence. He remained deep inside his bonded while Nai wrapped an arm around her. "You had to come to us. Of your own free will. It's the only way you would be able to give yourself to us both."

"But I hurt you." Amanda gazed up at Cade. Arctic ice-blue eyes watched her intently. "Both of you."

"Our love is strong, and we can both forgive you," Nai assured her.

"I want to bond now." Although Nai had one arm

wrapped around her, she kept her gaze on Cade. "More than anything in the entire world."

Cade broke eye contact with her and glanced at Nai. "Once we're bonded, there will be no more running and hiding. I won't have Nai hurt like she was." Although he didn't say it, Amanda knew she had also hurt him. "This is our forever. So choose wisely."

Don't leave us. The unspoken words, she heard them. Knew them. Breathed them. "I know. We can figure out everything later. It's not important. You and Nai are important. Our bond is important."

"Would you like to finish and then we can bond?" A shiver of anticipation rolled through her.

"As long as you join us. We both need you," Nai whispered, and, without hesitation, Amanda leaned down to kiss her. Soft, smooth lips mated with hers as Cade began to rock against Nai, who groaned.

Without waiting to be asked, Amanda cupped Nai's breast. Using her thumb and forefinger, she rolled the small, brown nipple over and over again as Cade began to pick his speed up. Breaking the kiss, Amanda shifted on the bed to allow Nai to dip her hand between her thighs.

"Ahh, my firebrand. Your pussy is sopping wet for us."

Cade grunted and pushed Nai's slim thighs farther apart. "Feed me her juices, Nai," he growled out as he leaned over her body while Amanda continued to suck on her nipple. "Fuck, she tastes amazing."

"Her pussy is mine at this moment." Nai gasped when Amanda released her nipple with a pop. "When you have made me scream your name in release, you may then drink from Amanda's nectar."

"A challenge, *hjarta*?"

"If you are willing, then, yes," Nai panted.

Cade changed their position so she could fit under her oracle's body. Once he began to move, Nai kissed the top of her sex.

"I believe your firebrand is craving your pussy, Nai." Cade shifted back and, without missing a beat, Amanda leaned forward and licked his glistening dick down to the root.

"Fuck. Do it again!" Cade demanded.

Instead, she moved to Nai's sex and flicked her swollen clit with her tongue. Her hands dug into Amanda's hair, and she gave a slight tug. Amanda groaned. A mix of pleasure and pain rolled through her body. Her turn would come once they were completed. Wanting to give Nai and Cade as much pleasure as she could, Amanda licked and lapped at both Cade's dick and Nai's pussy.

"I'm not going to last," he declared. "Turn around, Amanda, and let our *hjarta* feast on your pussy while I fuck her." She quickly obeyed then guided Nai's mouth down to her aching sex while Cade repositioned himself. Once Nai began to lick her pussy, he quickened his pace, which would push them over the edge.

"Come, Amanda. I want to taste you." Nai's tongue speared through her sex and began to tease and flick over her throbbing clit.

Amanda watched in fascination as Cade thrust in and out of Nai's pussy, while the woman continued to devour her. They worked in tandem like they were always supposed to be together. Each of them an extension of the other. The pureness of their coupling overwhelmed her. She closed her eyes, arching as intense pleasure raced through her.

"Yes!" Nai cried out at the same moment she sunk two trim fingers into Amanda's pussy.

"Shit...." Cade growled.

"Do I allow her to come again?" Nai panted while Cade's thrust became more erratic.

"No. I want her to come on my cock during our bonding," Cade grunted.

"I agree." Nai's tongue flicked over her clit.

"Make her work for it."

"As you wish." Nai gave a throaty chuckle.

They continued to assault her with pleasure. She withed against the bed, and all she could do was hold on for the ride. "Oh please." She whimpered. "I need."

"So damn pretty."

"Yes, she is. I need to come, *orm-am*. Please," she squealed.

Amanda took advantage of their crazy predicament. *Thank fuck, Nai had lube when it came to teasing Cade. the oracle has wicked talented fingers when she gets feisty.* She opened the cap and squirted some on her fingers. She knew how to blow both of their minds while her little mate kept her on edge with her tongue and fingers.

Amanda reached between them and probed his rear, gauging his reaction. When he hissed and his pace faltered, she knew she had him. Rimming his entrance, she teased the sensitive flesh. "Fuck," he groaned. "What are you doing to me?"

"Giving you pleasure," she said, then moaned when Nai sucked her clit into her mouth.

"Little human, you play with fire."

"Uh huh," she murmured, slipping her finger into him. She worked the digit in and out, matching his pace. "Feels good though, huh?"

"So fucking good."

"And when I do this?" She curled the appendage, rubbing the gland.

"Shit," he grunted. "You keep doing that and I'm coming."

"Okay," she answered. She continued circling his sweet spot. Her body tingled with arousal as his paced turned more urgent. The sounds they made were filled with pleasure, adding to the sensations crashing through her. "Come, Cade. Give it to her."

"*Hjarta* first," he muttered.

Nai stiffened, her back arched as her mouth came off Amanda. Their oracle's cry signaled Nai's release. Cade filled her once more, and he gripped Amanda's intrusion. Each pulse of his body sent an erotic thrill down her spine.

With a gentle ease, she withdrew from him, and he helped Nai climb out from beneath them. Aching and turned on, Amanda needed a minute to gather herself. Her head spun, and her heart hammered at the emotional overload battering her body. These two people forgave her.

Gave her a second chance.

The heaviness of the situation overwhelmed her. While Cade cradled Nai's body to his, she had to clean up a bit. She needed a moment to compose herself. This was it. In a few minutes she'd bind herself to those two people in the bedroom. Whereas she'd been afraid two days ago, today, resolve filled her. She had to do this. Had to take the leap. Had to make it right.

When he walked back into the room, Cade's Arctic-blue gaze landed on her. "You okay?" The trepidation laced through the question devastated her. He thought she'd run again.

"Yep," she said, crawling into bed beside him. "I had to get myself straight for this. Reconcile what is in my head and heart so I don't screw up ever again." She pressed her lips to his. "I'm sorry." She nuzzled his nose with hers. "I hurt you more than you're telling me, but I feel it. I need to fix this."

"Bond has to be without regret for it to work."

"I have no regrets and will never have any," she said, cupping his cheek. "My only regret is all the pain I caused you and Nai, but I will strive to make it up to both of you."

"Now, the time is right," Nai said, sitting up. "Now we must bond."

They clasped hands, once more, their bodies touching as they had the other night. The kiss would seal their mating. Their souls entwining would complete the bond. "I'm ready," Amanda said. "Kiss me."

"With pleasure, little human," he said.

Cade pressed his lips to hers and she sank into it. Their tongues tangled, as the air around them thickened with expectation. Electricity sizzled along her skin, causing the tiny hairs to stand up. As much as he gave, she returned, until the door to their souls opened then their souls touched. Nai's lips brushed both of theirs and, within seconds, all three of their bright white energies mingled, and then twirled together, locking as one.

The experience left her breathless and shaken. The amount of love, or pureness coursing through her bear and her oracle, astounded her. Her lips trembled but she didn't part from them. When the air settled and barrage of emotions assailing her ebbed, Cade pulled back. She sagged against him as heaving sobs tore through her body.

Encased in his heat, she curled into his body and cried. Behind her, Nai had joined them. She wrapped herself and one of her silk saris around them. "It is done. We are one," her oracle said. "Take what you need from him, firebrand."

She glanced up at Cade. The hungry look in his eyes, and the steely erection pressed to her hips, told everything she needed to know. He wanted her as much as she craved him.

Straddling his hips, he positioned himself at her entrance. Amanda lowered herself onto him, taking him on one thrust. Pain and pleasure coalesced into a ball of desire deep within her. She rolled her hips then set them in a mutually gratifying pace. Not too fast, but not too slow. She knew when the time was right he'd take over and give her exactly what she needed.

She grew more aroused with each passing second, until that determined gleam appeared in his eyes. He rolled them without effort, covering her body with his. His lips curled as he pushed even deeper into her. "Cade," she cried out.

"I've got you," he whispered, setting a brutal pace. "We've always got you."

Higher she climbed. With each shift of his hips, she came closer to her release. His body hummed with energy, adding to the emotional blanket wrapping around her. She fed off it. Taking all of their positive life forces into herself. She was nourished by it, basked in it, and knew she was loved. When his finger skimmed over her clit, she detonated, coming apart in his arms. And, seconds later, he joined her roaring through his release.

Covered in a fine shine of sweat, her heart thudding in her ears, she knew she was finally home.

"I love you both, so much," she whispered, while trying to catch her breath. "Wherever you go, I go."

Nai gave a small chuckle. "We're not going far, firebrand."

Cade rolled them so she fit into the crook of his body while Nai situated herself on his other side. "We're not?"

"No," she said. "I have accepted an offer to stay here and help Sage."

"You mean it?" Amanda asked.

"Yes," Cade answered. "But the question remains, what are you going to do? Is Para Elite something you can live without?"

She figured it out while staying holed up in her room. She'd only needed Para Elite because she didn't have a family and they fit the bill. Now, since she had Cade and Nai, she didn't need the team. "I already turned in my retirement papers last night. As of 8:00 a.m., I am a free woman. You're my family now. If you're staying here, then so am I."

"Thank fuck." Cade growled. Leaning in, he pressed his lips to hers. "Ready for round three?"

Nai laughed. "I think we've created a monster."

"I wouldn't have it any other way."